SOUL STEALER

The Alchemist's Son

SOUL STEALER
Martin Booth

LITTLE, BROWN AND COMPANY
New York ⌁ Boston

Matt

Text copyright © 2003 by Martin Booth
First U.S. hardcover edition published by Little, Brown and Company in 2005
First published in Great Britain by Puffin Books in 2003
Reader's Guide copyright © 2006 by Little, Brown and Company

Little, Brown and Company

Hachette Book Group USA
1271 Avenue of the Americas, New York, NY 10020
Visit our Web site at www.lb-kids.com

First paperback edition: September 2006

Library of Congress Cataloging-in-Publication Data

Booth, Martin
Soul stealer / by Martin Booth. — 1ST U.S. ed.
p.   cm. — (The alchemist's son ; pt. 2)
Summary: Pip and her twin brother, Tim, join forces again with Sebastian, the
alchemist's son they awakened from a centuries-long slumber, to fight against an
evil magician who learns people's deepest secrets in order to control their souls.
ISBN 0-316-15591-8 (HC)
ISBN-13 978-0-316-05993-0 (PB)
ISBN-10 0-316-05993-5 (PB)
[1. Alchemy — Fiction.   2. Magic — Fiction.   3. Brothers and sisters —
Fiction.   4. Twins — Fiction.   5. Adventure and adventurers — Fiction.
6. England — Fiction.]   I. Title.   II. Series: Booth, Martin. Alchemist's son.
pt. 2. PZ7.B6468So 2005 [Fic] — dc22
2004057728

10 9 8 7 6 5 4 3 2 1

Q-MT

Printed in the United States of America

The text was set in Bembo, and the display type is Tagliente.

For my family — Alex, Emma and my wife,
Helen — who helped beat back my own demon
in order to write this story

Contents

SOUL STEALER

Martin Booth says: All the magic in *Soul Stealer* is real: the chants, the herbs, the potions and the equipment. The colophon ⊙ used in this book is an ancient alchemical sign referring to the *caput mortuum*, a death's head or skull: it symbolizes decay and decline. It is, even today, still used as a common curse in southern Italy and the Balkans. The other colophon ⚭ is the alchemical symbol for *aurum potabile* or liquid gold, which was thought to be a youth-giving potion or the elixir of life.

Alchemy, a curious blend of magic and science, was the chemistry of the Middle Ages. People who studied alchemy were called alchemists and they devoted their lives to the quest for the elixir of life, the creation of a homunculus (an artificial man) and the means to turn ordinary (or ignoble) metal, like iron or lead, into a noble metal, like gold or silver. This was known as transmutation, a term also used in nuclear science to mean the conversion of one element into another, either naturally or by artificial means.

One

The Eye of Innocence and Experience

Pip opened her eyes and looked blearily at her alarm clock. The digital numbers flicked over to read 6:57 a.m. She slowly sat up, stretched and, pushing the curtains aside without getting out of bed, peered out of the window. A thin veil of river mist hung over the fields surrounding the old manor house of Rawne Barton, the trees outlined against the gray light like the veins in skeletal leaves. The hills in the distance were barely visible, the quarry little more than a faint dark scar upon them. A robin settled momentarily on the window sill, puffed out its orange breast, chirped once and flitted off. She loved these early moments when she was still half asleep and the world, like her, had not yet fully woken up.

Yet, somewhere in the pit of her stomach, she felt a gnawing apprehension which at first she could not place. Then, gradually, she realized the cause of it. This was to be the first day of term, a new term in a new school — and a secondary school, at that.

Reaching for the window, Pip opened the latch. A cool, damp drift of air filtered into the room. It smelled of the first falling leaves of autumn and the grass her father had mown the day before. Feeling its chill, she snuggled back down under the duvet, preserving the last vestiges of warmth.

Suddenly, through the open window, Pip heard a noise. It sounded bizarrely like an animal roaring somewhere far off, followed by someone clicking heavy sticks together. The hair went up on the back of her neck. It was an unearthly sound, echoing in the mist yet also muffled by it. It was unlike anything she had ever heard before.

As she slipped quickly out of bed, Pip's toes curled with fear as they felt for her slippers. She was afraid, yet at the same time, intensely curious. The noises had to have a rational explanation, had to be made by an animal of some sort and yet, at the same time, she could think of no wild animals in England that, outside of a zoo, even remotely roared.

As she stood up, the noise ceased abruptly. Pip wondered if she had simply imagined it, that it was nothing more than a remnant of the last dream she had had before waking. In recent weeks, her dreams had become quite vivid and fantastical. This, she considered to herself, was hardly surprising after the events of the summer holidays. . . . Indeed, after them, if there were a saber-toothed tiger loose in the English countryside, released by some evil force or twisted mind, she would not have been at all amazed.

A moment later, her alarm clock went off. Pip tapped the snooze button and, standing in her slippers, turned towards the chair where her mother had laid out her new school uniform the night before — a yellow-and-blue striped tie, a white shirt, a gray sweater and a gray pleated skirt.

The second she took her first step towards the chair, however, Pip froze and then spun around. In the half-light across the other side of her bedroom stood the vague, shadowy silhouette of a person, half hidden by the angle of her wardrobe. She sharply sucked in her breath. The hair on her neck and arms prickled. She felt her hands go immediately clammy and the blood drain from her cheeks. Almost as a reflex, she looked around for a weapon, but all she could see was her badminton racket.

"Fear not. It is I," said the outline, softly.

"Sebastian!" Pip retorted, angrily.

Sebastian stepped into the middle of the room. He was wearing a dark, nondescript cloak draped over his shoulders.

"You scared the living daylights out of me," Pip complained.

"I apologize most humbly," Sebastian replied with a short bow. "It was not my intention to startle."

"Well, you did!" Pip snapped back.

Aware that her midriff was showing, she smoothed down her pajama top to below her waist and rubbed her arms to remove the goose pimples.

Pip and her twin brother, Tim, had met Sebastian during the summer holidays. Knowing him had led them into a remarkable and perilous adventure. They had soon

3

discovered that Sebastian was no ordinary boy. For one thing, he was more or less six hundred years old but had been in a kind of hibernation for most of the time. Moreover, he possessed alchemical powers learned from his father, an alchemist of repute.

Rawne Barton had been built by Sebastian's father on land granted by the King. It was rightfully his home. Still, Pip considered, this did not give him the right to sneak about her bedroom whenever he chose.

"In your time, was it common courtesy to enter a lady's bedroom in the middle of the night?" Pip demanded; then she grinned and added, "What are you doing here anyway, skulking about like this?"

"It is morn," Sebastian pointed out, "not night but, yes, decorum would not have had me linger in your chamber. However," he added matter-of-factly, "I see it my place to guard you through the dark hours. From time to time, I look upon you to ensure you are safe."

"You mean you stand here while I'm sleeping?" Pip replied, somewhat taken aback by the thought.

"Not just you. I watch over Tim, also."

"Does he know?" Pip asked.

"He knows not," Sebastian answered, "for I do not remain in a solitary position. A sentry who does not patrol the entire castle is not fulfilling his duty."

Pip picked up her hairbrush and started to tug at her sleep-tousled hair.

"Well, it's day now so I don't need guarding. And I've got to get up and dressed. So, if you don't mind . . ."

From across the fields came another curt, grunting roar. Pip glanced at the window.

"As for that sound which alerted you, be not concerned," Sebastian said. "It is but that of two red deer stags. My father used to hunt them here with the King. Autumn is coming and they are in rut, the stags fighting over the hinds. Although England is much changed from my father's time, there are still some such creatures in the woods and wilder places. See."

Sebastian pointed to the window. Outlined against the mist down by the river, Pip could make out two magnificent stags, standing as if to attention with their antlers branched into the air. Facing each other against the backdrop of the early morning light, they might have been posing for the painting of a heraldic shield. As she watched, they lowered their heads, briefly clashed their antlers together then, separating, walked sedately off in different directions, to be swallowed by the fog.

"That was fantastic!" Pip exclaimed. "I didn't know such amazing animals lived around here."

"They are dignified beasts," Sebastian declared. "They come down from the moorland to the woods. One usually espies them only at dusk and first light, for they are shy creatures."

"Look," Pip went on, turning her back on Sebastian and continuing to brush her hair. "I don't think we need a security guard. The house has an alarm system for Dad's cameras and computers and stuff. If it's triggered, lights flash, a siren sounds and the security firm gets an alert call."

Sebastian made no immediate reply. There was a soft footfall in the corridor, and the bedroom door opened.

"As usual," said Pip with resignation and without even bothering to glance over her shoulder. "You'll never learn to knock, will you, Tim?"

"Sorry, sis," said Tim, coming in and pushing the door behind him. He was already dressed in his school uniform. "Up and ready?"

"Do I look it?" Pip answered sarcastically.

It was at that moment Tim noticed Sebastian standing in the room. "Hey! What're you doing here?"

Sebastian made no immediate reply. Tim gave his sister a quizzical look, quickly raising and lowering his eyebrows. She glowered back. From the end of the corridor came their mother's voice. "Breakfast!"

Their father's voice followed. "Shake a leg, you two! Bourne End Comprehensive school throws its doors wide open for you. The spectacular light of secondary education shines forth to greet you to the future of academe!"

Pip and Tim exchanged glances. *Spectacular* was one of their father's favorite words. Sebastian came across the room.

"I must have a word with you before you depart," he announced and, from a pocket in his cloak, he removed a thin, gold chain from which hung a tiny pendant set with a cloudy white stone. He held it out to Pip. "I wish you to take this and wear it at all times, especially when away from Rawne Barton."

"Thank you," said Pip, taken aback with what she assumed was a present. "It's very pretty."

Tim winked at Pip and raised his eyebrows again. She cast him another dirty look in return, yet she did feel flattered.

"This is not a gift," Sebastian announced solemnly as he hung the chain around Pip's neck, securing the clasp, "nor is it mere ornamentation. It is called the Eye of Innocence and Experience and belonged originally to Queen Joan."

"Queen Joan?" Tim repeated.

He had heard of Queen Elizabeth, Queen Victoria and Queen Anne, even Queen Boudicca, but Queen Joan? The name, he thought, did not exactly have the right regal ring to it. He and Pip had a great-aunt called Joan, and she was an evil old woman.

"Joan of Navarre," Sebastian explained, "was the wife of King Henry the Fourth of England. When the King was absent fighting in France," Sebastian went on, "she was accused by her enemies at court of witchcraft and of trying to kill him by magic. She was arrested and cast into a dungeon."

"And they executed her?" Tim guessed.

"No," Sebastian replied, "she was released when the King returned and showed that the pendant had protected him."

"That must mean the King wore it in battle . . ." Tim said.

Sebastian nodded.

"Cool!" Tim exclaimed.

"How did you get it?" Pip asked.

"My grandfather fashioned it for the Queen in the year of Our Lord 1400. She later returned it to him, for she became afraid of its ability."

Pip looked down at the pendant where it hung against her skin. It seemed utterly incredible that she was wearing a piece of magical jewelry once owned by a fifteenth-century queen of England and carried by the King into battle.

"What do you mean, its ability?" Pip repeated. She was beginning to feel apprehensive herself.

"So," Tim said, "all your family were alchemists then, not just your father?"

Sebastian chose to ignore the questions but smiled faintly and said, "Study well the gemstone. At this moment it is murky, but there will be times when it is crystal clear. It may also shiver. At that moment, you must be especially aware."

Eight weeks earlier, both Pip and Tim would have treated this remark with considerable cynicism and wondered which computer games Sebastian had been playing. Yet, after all they had gone through together, they now knew better.

"Aware of what?" Tim asked.

"One cannot say," Sebastian replied, enigmatically. "Accept just that it will warn you of close danger, for it has seen much evil itself and has absorbed much understanding and learning thereby."

"Better wear it in math class," Tim advised with a smirk. "Not your strongest subject, sis."

Sebastian looked askance at Tim. "It will not provide solutions to problems," he said, "but only give caution of matters beyond your perception."

"Shall we really need it?" Pip ventured, ignoring Tim's attempt at humor. "I mean de Loudéac's gone and . . ."

"You are stepping into a new world," Sebastian replied.

"It's a new school," Tim rejoined, "not a new planet.

We've already seen the headmaster. He's definitely not the spawn of Satan."

Sebastian said casually, "Appearances can be deceptive. It is ever best to be prepared for any eventuality."

"Come on! Shake those legs!" their father shouted from the bottom of the stairs.

Pip held the pendant up. It weighed, she reckoned, barely five grams and seemed almost to float in the air above her palm.

"One more thing," Sebastian added. "It is just for you and Tim. Share it not with others. Keep it suspended within your clothing."

"If Pip keeps it hidden, how will we know when it changes?" Tim asked.

"You will know," Sebastian replied, adding, "May your day be bright."

With that, he turned and left the room. The last they saw of him was the corner of his cloak sweeping around the door.

"Do I detect the heady perfume of romance in the air?" Tim ventured.

"No!" Pip retorted sharply. "You do not! And if you would now get out, I can get dressed." She pushed Tim through the door and shut it firmly behind him.

As they sat facing each other at breakfast, Pip and Tim were silent, thinking not so much of the daunting prospect of starting at secondary school but of what had happened during the summer.

It seemed quite incredible that, since leaving their junior school in June, they had changed homes, and had discovered and been befriended by the centuries-old son of an alchemist. Even more amazing was the fact that Sebastian had been kept alive through the centuries in order to foil the evil of de Loudéac, his father's enemy — and now they were also involved. They had helped to stop de Loudéac from creating a homunculus — an artificial man — which persisted in giving Pip nightmares.

She looked up at her mother, standing by the toaster, removing the crumb tray and shaking it out over the sink. What, Pip wondered, would her parents think if they knew they had bought a house once owned by the royal court alchemist to King Henry the Fifth of England, who had been burned at the stake in the field outside and whose six-centuries-old son lived in a laboratory in the bowels of the earth beneath the building, approached by a secret passage from their daughter's bedroom?

Pip's thoughts were broken by the sound of her father's car starting up. That morning, he was leaving for a business meeting concerning his television production company and was going to take them to school on their first day.

"Hurry up, you two!" their mother goaded them as she started to gather the breakfast plates and load them into the dishwasher, pushing two lunch boxes across the kitchen table.

Gathering up her school bag, Pip pondered in passing what her mother would say if she discovered the house was being protected not just by an alarm system panel between the fridge and the back door, but also by Sebastian, her children's new friend who wandered through the house at night, somehow avoiding setting off the movement sensors in the downstairs rooms.

"What're you working on now, Dad?" Tim inquired as they drove towards the school, which was on the outskirts of the nearby large market town of Exington.

"You really want to know, Timbo?" his father said.

"Yes," Tim replied, "and I'm not five any more. Let's drop the Timbo handle."

"Sounds like a dog food," Pip added.

"It is," their father replied. "Comes on the market next month."

"And I've you to thank for this?" Tim asked, mortified by the thought.

Mr. Ledger just grinned.

"If this ever gets out," Tim threatened Pip, "the world will know your middle name."

To defuse the situation, their father went on, "I'm actually working on the promotion of a new store loyalty card."

"What's it called?"

"The Kard. With a K."

"Krap name!" Tim declared. "With a K."

"Aren't you ever going to do music videos?" Pip asked longingly.

Ahead, a pupil in a Bourne End Comprehensive uniform was walking by the side of the road. He was stocky and looked scruffy, his clothing creased. He moved in a vaguely apelike fashion.

"I didn't know your school took in pupils from the monkey house," Mr. Ledger quipped.

Two

Zombie Frogs and Dead Cows' Eyes

The school day began with all the pupils lined up in the main hall. On the stage, in front of an oak table which displayed an impressive array of sporting cups and shields, stood the headmaster, Dr. Singall.

"Welcome, everybody," he announced, "either upon your return to Bourne End Comprehensive or into its ranks for the first time. I trust we all have a happy and rewarding term ahead of us. Our academic results in the summer exams were our best yet and we look forward to going from strength to strength in the future."

He waved his hand in the direction of the trophies. "As you can see, we also have a great field of sporting excellence here. And our congratulations go out to Stephen Wroxall who has, during the summer, won the All-England Under-Fifteen Marathon." At this point, his speech was interrupted by loud applause.

"However," Dr. Singall continued as the clapping died away, "school is more than winning cups and passing exams. It is also the forging of your futures, molding the person you are to be throughout your life through friendship, consideration for others, diligence, hard work and, dare I say it, hard play." He looked around the hall to where the staff, accompanied by the school prefects, were lining the sides, standing beneath photographs of various school plays or victorious sporting teams. "We all welcome you, myself and the entire staff. For those of you who are new, it will be a puzzling first few weeks, but bear with us. You will soon feel at home in the community which is Bourne End Comprehensive."

At that, he stepped aside, and the deputy headmistress took over, reading out the bulletin. When this was done, the teachers stepped forward to gather their individual classes, picking out each line that was to be their homeroom and taking them around the school to their various bases. Pip and Tim found themselves in a line of Year Sevens being led towards the science wing, where the classrooms were filled with scientific equipment and furnished with stools and workbenches rather than chairs and desks. The specific room into which they were taken was, according to the sign on the door, *Chemistry Laboratory One*.

The class filed in silently, looking around. Some of the pupils were clearly awestruck by the sight of the scientific apparatus. The wide workbenches were lined with retorts, bottles of common laboratory chemicals or reagents in central wooden and metal racks. Tripods and Bunsen burners stood in rows beside polished brass gas taps and, every meter or so, there was a white porcelain sink with two brass taps arching over it. Whereas in many of the classrooms the floors were made of wood, in this room they were made of hard formica tiles, many of them stained where chemicals had been spilled on them over the years. Along the walls were glass-fronted cabinets filled with jars and tins of chemicals and equipment such as beakers, racks of test tubes and white electronic chemical scales.

The pupils shuffled about and sat down on the stools behind the benches. The teacher they had followed there stood behind the large demonstration bench, which was slightly higher than the pupils'. Behind it, set into the wall next to a very large whiteboard, was a fume cupboard with glass doors and sides and a silver foil-lined chimney flue leading up from a hood in the center towards an extractor fan in the ceiling. Through the fume cupboard could be seen the next-door preparation room where experiments could be made ready. Like the classroom, it too was lined with cabinets of chemicals and equipment. To the left rear of the demonstration desk was the door into this inner sanctum, a label stuck to its single glass panel reading starkly: *Absolutely No Entry to Pupils.*

"Good morning," the teacher greeted them when everyone was settled and looking in his direction. "My name is Mr. Yoland. I am the head of chemistry. This is my laboratory but it is also your homeroom and, for as long as it is your home base, you must be . . ." he looked around the class, his eyes passing from face to face, ". . . *exceedingly* careful in here. These chemicals are dangerous, many of them are poisonous, and you must not touch anything without my express permission. Furthermore," he added curtly, "much of the equipment is very expensive and I will not — I repeat, not! — condone breakage."

Pip and Tim looked briefly at each other. This was not what they had expected. In junior school, the classrooms were cozy places, almost friendly, the walls decorated with pictures, murals, friezes and project folders. This room was, in stark contrast to all they had known before, foreboding. Yet both of them were excited by the prospect of what lay ahead. As for their new homeroom teacher, he was clearly a very strict and stern man, yet the reason for his brusqueness was obvious to both of them. The laboratory was indeed a dangerous place, and it was clear that there had to be rigorous rules governing it for safety, if nothing else.

"There will be no running or playing the fool in this room," Mr. Yoland went on. "Bags may only be brought in at the start or end of the day. No food or drink may be consumed here, and you are not allowed access during break or lunchtime unless I or another teacher is present. Is this implicitly understood?"

The class nodded in respectful silence.

"If a rain break is announced and you are excluded from the playground, you do not return here under any circumstances, but you go directly to the dining hall. Understood?"

Everyone again nodded their agreement and understanding.

"Now," Mr. Yoland pointed to the door, "down the corridor on the left you will find your lockers. They already have your names on them and I suggest you all go and acquaint yourselves with where they are positioned. Put your bags and coats in them, then return here. You may secure the locker doors only with combination padlocks, the setting of which is to be any year that is memorable for you. It might be your birth year or, much better, one of your parents' or grandparents' years of birth or a famous year in history like 1066. This will prevent you from forgetting your individual combinations. Any questions?" No one responded so the teacher continued, "If you forget the number and the custodian is obliged to cut your lock free, there will be a charge of £2.50 for this service. These locks may be purchased from the school office. No other types will be permitted. We won't have any chatter. Off you go."

Everybody filed out, Pip following Tim.

"I wonder what Sebastian would make of our homeroom," Pip murmured. Yet no sooner had she spoken than she sensed someone watching her. She glanced over her shoulder, half expecting to see Mr. Yoland looking at her, but he was in the laboratory. Behind her in the corridor only other pupils mingled.

As Tim and Pip reached the rank of lockers, another Year Seven boy came up to them. He was short and scrubby with a thick neck and large hands which were out of proportion to the length of his arms. His small ears seemed to come out from the top of his neck rather than from the side of his head, and his salt-and-pepper-colored hair was close-shaven. He was, Pip thought, one of the most unsavory-looking boys she had ever seen. Tim recognized him as the boy they had observed walking along the road.

"You!" the boy bluntly addressed Tim. "What junior school have you come from?"

"We just moved here," Tim replied. "You wouldn't know it."

"And you!" the boy said curtly, addressing Pip. "What about you?"

"That's my sister," Tim told him.

Ignoring this information, the boy went on, "And where have you moved to?"

"Well, if it's any business of yours," interrupted Pip, who was becoming intensely annoyed by the boy's rudeness, "we've moved to Rawne Barton."

Pausing for a moment as if considering this information, the boy then turned on his heel and walked abruptly away.

"That was the Neanderthal we passed on the road," Tim said.

"His name's Scrotton," said a boy standing next to them, "Guy Scrotton. He was in our junior school. You want to watch out for him. He's a nasty piece of work. He's a bully," the boy went on. "Sucks up to teachers, too. Rats on you. He's a real little dung ball."

Once they had found their lockers, Pip and Tim returned to the laboratory, where Mr. Yoland was still standing behind the demonstration bench.

"Right," he said as the class filed back in once more, "please be seated." He opened a foolscap register book and took out from his inner jacket pocket a fountain pen with a gold cap. "When I call your surname, I'd like you to come out to my desk one by one and give me your home address, home telephone number, parents' work addresses and telephone numbers if you know them."

As she waited for her name to be called, Pip noticed,

lingering in the air, a faint but obnoxious odor which irritated her nostrils.

Rubbing her nose, she whispered to Tim, "Can you smell something?"

Thinking of de Loudéac's alias — Malodor, which meant "bad smell" — she snuck a look at the pendant. It was milky, as if a tiny waft of gray smoke were trapped in it. The discoloration put her mind at ease.

"Smells like rotten eggs," Tim muttered.

A girl sitting on the next stool whispered, "We had a science lesson here on a registration day last term. It's a gas called hydrogen sulphide."

"Well," Tim replied quietly, grinning at her, "that's chemistry for you," and, turning to Pip, added, "if there's going to be a room that smells odd, it's either going to be this one or the boys' locker rooms. Like in the junior school, sweaty socks, manky underwear and wet pullovers that stink like damp dogs."

"You know, Tim," Pip murmured, "you can be really crude at times."

Tim's response was to softly hum the opening bars of *The Simpsons'* theme tune and grin. This grin, however, soon disappeared when, on looking up, he saw Mr. Yoland watching him intently, one eyebrow critically raised, the other eye narrowed disapprovingly.

"If you wish to sing, young man," he said tersely, "kindly go to the music department."

"Yes, sir," Tim replied, guiltily.

After another few seconds of pointedly staring at Tim, Mr. Yoland turned his attention back to registering the students.

Eventually, Pip's name was called and she found herself standing before Mr. Yoland.

"Phillipa Ledger?" he inquired.

"Yes, sir," Pip confirmed.

"Address?"

"Rawne Barton, sir," Pip answered.

At this piece of information, Mr. Yoland briefly looked up from the register. The daylight from the laboratory window seemed momentarily to glint in his eye. As if at the back of his eye, Pip could make out what appeared to be another reflection, of a tall, thin, wavering, narrow flame with a cold, blue conical core dancing in a gentle breeze. She turned to see if, on one of the benches, there was a Bunsen burner alight: yet there was not. None were connected to a gas tap, and most of the equipment was neatly stored away as it must have been throughout the summer holidays.

"Really?" Mr. Yoland remarked. "A very fine old house. Fifteenth century, I believe, with quite a fascinating past. We have had a number of very successful school history field trips there. If I recall correctly, there are some most interesting Roman remains in the grounds. Tell me, Phillipa, what is your father's occupation?"

"He makes television commercials," Pip replied. "He works from home."

"Fascinating! Most fascinating!" Mr. Yoland glanced at his homeroom list and looked up at Tim, continuing, "and that, I assume, is your musically inclined brother, Timothy?"

"Yes," Pip confirmed.

As the teacher spoke, Pip felt a faint trembling

against her chest, as if a mobile phone was going off against her skin. She touched the pendant through the material of her shirt. It was quivering.

Mr. Yoland entered Tim's name in the register and, with an old-fashioned brass and wood scientific ruler, drew several short lines and some ditto marks beside it. Pip noticed how precise and neat his writing appeared. The ink in his pen was sepia, the color of old documents or faded photographs.

As Pip turned to go back to her stool, she found the trembling ceased but the flame she had seen in Mr. Yoland's eye remained in her own, the shifting image temporarily burned into her retina. At the same time, a faint perfume seemed to come from the teacher as if he was wearing a strong aftershave scented with thyme and lemon blossom.

When the registration process was finished, course timetables and maps of the school were handed out. The class was then dismissed to find the rooms in which they would be taught.

It was a large school, but well ordered. All the subject rooms were labeled — even the custodian's office and store, full of mops, industrial vacuum cleaners, buckets and tins of polish bore a sign reading *Janitor*. Some of the classrooms were big: the geography room had a massive globe hanging from the ceiling, while the history room had cabinets full of displays of stone tools and old bottles with diagrams and pictures of famous battles hanging on the walls. In the IT room were ranks of PCs and printers. The design and technology workshops contained planing machines, a circular saw and a bandsaw, wood and metal-turning lathes, a forge and several anvils — and an old Mini Metro in pieces. The art room had rows of easels, pottery wheels and a kiln for firing clay. The biology laboratory was lined with racks and shelves of preserved specimens in jars — pickled frogs and newts, a dissected chicken, a cow's head that had been sliced in half lengthways so that one could see the interior. There were even some cows' eyes in one jar that stared out disconcertingly from within a murky liquid.

The gymnasium was particularly impressive: it contained a wide range of equipment from blue crash mats to indoor cricket nets, climbing bars and ropes, parallel bars, benches, a trampoline and several vaulting horses.

At break time, Pip and Tim followed all the other pupils out into the playground. Most of the new Year Seven pupils stuck together in a large mass, talking to friends whom they had known in their junior schools but, as Pip and Tim knew no one, they kept themselves to themselves. Scrotton, they noticed, also tended not to mix.

"What do you reckon to the place?" Pip asked her brother.

"Pretty impressive," Tim replied.

"And what do you think of Mr. Yoland?" she continued. "I bet, when he started teaching, they still caned you and he wore a black gown like some emaciated Batman."

"And I bet," Tim added, "he's not someone to mess with, either."

Shortly before the bell went for them to return to their classroom, the boy Scrotton approached again, sidling up to them with an irritating smirk on his face.

"You any good at chemistry?" he asked Tim forth-rightly.

"No, not really," Tim admitted. "I've never done it before and neither's my sister. We didn't have real science courses in junior school."

"Huh! I am," Scrotton said dismissively, grunting and strutting off, pushing another boy out of his way as he went.

As he walked away, Pip said quietly, "He smells a bit."

"Only a bit!" Tim agreed. "It's definitely time he shook hands with Mr. Soap."

"And became acquainted with Mrs. Toothpaste," Pip added, "but it's not just BO or bad breath," she went on. "He smells sort of . . ." She searched for an apt word, ". . . earthy."

"Who cares?" Tim said. "We'll just give him a wide berth. He'll sort himself out in time and we can ignore him. It's a big school — there must be at least two hundred in Year Seven alone. We don't have to come across him if we don't want to."

Back in the chemistry laboratory, more formalities were completed. Scrotton came and sat around the corner of the bench, close to Tim. From there, he kept looking at him, as if studying him or trying to catch his eye to engage him in conversation. Every now and then he cast a quick look in Mr. Yoland's direction. The teacher, save just once when he briefly acknowledged Scrotton's look, ignored him. Tim similarly did his best to pay him no attention.

When the lunchtime bell rang, Pip and Tim collected their food from their lockers and followed everyone else to a huge room marked *Dining Hall*. At one end was a counter selling cartons of juice or milk, soft drinks, biscuits, sweets, fruit, salad boxes and pre-packed sandwiches. Down the center were rows of plastic tables and chairs. Pip and Tim chose a table and sat down, opening their lunch boxes. They had just started to eat when Scrotton approached them and positioned himself across the table. He did not appear to have any food.

"What have you got?" he inquired.

"Sandwiches," Pip said.

"What's in 'em?" Scrotton demanded.

Tim kicked Pip's ankle under the table, but he was too late.

"Cheese and tomato," she replied.

"Give me one. I forgot mine," Scrotton retorted.

"No," said Tim firmly. "If you want something, go and buy it."

"Forgot me money," Scrotton answered.

"Tough!" Tim exclaimed and he purposefully bit into his first sandwich, holding it so that Scrotton could see it and adding, "Mine're Marmite and lettuce."

Scrotton gave them both a sneer and walked away to disappear among the tables.

"Charming!" Pip exclaimed.

"Every school's got one," Tim observed.

For the remainder of the day, Pip and Tim visited all their different subject teachers. In each classroom, they were given sets of text and exercise books. They gathered them all up and put them in their lockers. For one period, they were separated to be placed into groups for games and PE.

The last period of the day involved returning to the

chemistry laboratory to be dismissed by Mr. Yoland, who stood by the door as they filed out.

Walking past the teacher, Pip momentarily felt the strangest sensation. Although he was standing at least two meters from her with his arms folded across his chest, looking down the corridor at the other departing pupils, she somehow felt he was reaching out towards her. It was, she thought, as if she was going through a sort of magnetic field which was attracting every cell in her body, tingling every muscle and tugging at every nerve. A meter behind Mr. Yoland stood Scrotton, ostensibly rummaging in a grubby sports bag yet watching her intently at the same time.

"Well, kids, how's your day been?" asked Mr. Ledger as they got into his car.

"It's a huge school," Tim said. "Lots of equipment and stuff. Not like the junior school at all."

"No," said Mr. Ledger. "This is the real thing. Secondary education. Learning in the raw! No more playing in the sandpit, sitting on the story mat, cuddling Georgie the gerbil and eating the play dough."

"Do you have any idea at all what we actually did in junior school, Dad?" Pip inquired.

For a moment, Mr. Ledger took his eyes off the road ahead and grinned broadly at them over the back of the driver's seat.

"Not a clue," he said and he winked.

Immediately after tea, Pip and Tim went up to their rooms, arranged their school books on their bedroom shelves and changed out of their uniforms. Pip then sat on her bed and, with Tim at her side, leaned towards the wall, giving a few tentative taps on the wooden paneling. For a moment, there was silence before she and Tim could just discern the distant sound of Sebastian coming up through the wall, rising along the secret passage from his place under the ground.

Over the weeks, since their battle with de Loudéac, they had seen little of Sebastian. A few times, they had caught sight of him in the distance, down by the river, usually in the evening, a solitary figure slowly walking along the bank deep in thought, his hands thrust behind his back. Twice, he had turned away from the river and come up to the house, but he had not stayed long and had said very little. When Pip asked him what he was thinking about, he was reticent and remarked only that, despite their vanquishing of de Loudéac, he still felt ill at ease and the *aqua soporiferum*, the potion that induced sleep, would not yet let him fall into a deep slumber. This, he continued, was a sign that something remained amiss, although he could not identify it. When Tim had asked if he was worried that Malodor might return, he had evaded the question and simply said there remained much evil abroad in the world.

Sebastian soon materialized in Pip's bedroom, climbing out from behind the panel in the wall and closing it behind him.

"Has your day been a good day?" he inquired, sitting cross-legged on the floor before Pip and Tim. "How is your new school?"

"Big," Tim replied. "It must have at least a thousand pupils and over fifty teachers."

"We've got the head of chemistry as our homeroom teacher," Pip added.

"Strange guy," Tim went on. "He's got the hearing of a bat. I hummed something and he picked it up at five meters. Bit strict, but then we're in his laboratory for a homeroom, so I suppose he has to be."

"There's more to him than that," Pip went on. "He's creepy. When he looks at you, you get the feeling he's sort of studying you."

"Really," Sebastian replied thoughtfully, adding, "describe him to me."

Tim conjured up a mental picture of the teacher. "He's tall," he began, "thin, long bony fingers. Brown hair going gray. Weird haircut. Bald on top. Sticks out at the sides. A bit like Krusty the Clown's, only not green."

Sebastian looked nonplussed. "Never mind," Pip said, "you won't have heard of Krusty."

"Quite a pointed nose," Tim continued.

"With hairs sprouting from the nostrils," Pip cut in. "Earholes are pretty hairy, too."

"Of what age would you consider him?" Sebastian asked.

"Mid-fifties," Tim guessed, continuing, "pale skin, large ears."

"And his eyes?" Sebastian inquired.

An involuntary shudder ran down Pip's back. Something told her this interrogation was taking a nasty turn.

"Dark," she reported. "Sort of deep. The light from the window reflected in them," she paused, "as if there was a flame burning way down inside him, in the middle of his head. And," she went on, "he uses a strong aftershave."

"Of herbs and citrus fruit?" Sebastian asked.

Another ripple of fear ran down Pip's spine.

"Yes," she nodded and said, "thyme and lemons."

"It was not as you suppose a balm for shaving," Sebastian continued. "It was the scent of a pomander."

"A what?" Tim replied.

"In my father's time," Sebastian explained, "it was believed that noxious odors caused disease and, if one could counteract them with a pleasant smell, the risk of infection was much reduced. Thus people carried lemons and such fruit with them, often pierced with cloves, to produce a strong and beneficial scent. Of course, only the wealthy were able to do this, for such fruit were both rare and costly."

"Sort of like aromatherapy," Pip remarked. "Did it work?"

"No," Sebastian said bluntly, "it did not. One cannot control sickness merely with vapors."

"At the end of the day," Pip went on, "as we were dismissed, I had the strangest feeling. Going past him, I had the impression he was sort of magnetizing me. He wasn't looking at me and he wasn't close, and yet . . ."

"And the pendant?" Sebastian inquired.

"I couldn't look at it much without drawing attention to it," Pip admitted, "but, during registration, it vibrated."

A realization began to dawn on Tim.

"Are you saying," he asked Sebastian, "that our homeroom teacher . . . ?"

"Finally," Sebastian continued, ignoring him, "in your class, is there a boy of diminutive stature who seems quite objectionable?"

It was Tim's turn to nod.

"And his name, dare I hazard," Sebastian added, "is Guy Scratton."

"Scrotton," Tim corrected him. "Guy Scrotton."

"Time changes words," Sebastian replied, adding pensively, "and I would wager the master's name is Yoland."

"Yes," Tim confirmed in a voice little louder than a trembling whisper.

"You mean you know them?" Pip asked incredulously, a feeling of intense dread welling up through her entire body as if she were being filled with liquid fear.

"In a manner of speaking," Sebastian answered. "Let us say I was once acquainted with them, many years ago."

"Hang on!" Tim exclaimed. "Are you telling us Scrotton and Yoland're like you, six hundred and something years old?"

"And they can hibernate like you?" Pip asked.

"No," replied Sebastian. "They are both ignorant of *aqua soporiferum* which permits me, as you put it, to hibernate. Only I possess that knowledge, handed down to me by my father. Yet do you recall," he went on, "the threefold aims of alchemy, of which I have informed you?"

"Make a homunculus, turn common metals into gold, and achieve immortality," Tim said.

"The latter," Sebastian added, "was to be done by the discovery of the *elixir vitae*, or elixir of life, otherwise known as *aurum potabile*, or liquid gold. Yoland has clearly obtained an elixir, but it seems not to be the actual potion, for he continues to age, if slowly."

"And Scrotton also has a sip of this brew off and on?" Tim surmised.

"Indeed, no," Sebastian retorted. "Scrotton has no need of the elixir. He simply does not die."

"Like yeah!" Tim retorted. "That's impossible. Everything living dies at some time."

"On the contrary," Sebastian said. "Scrotton has already died, long ago, and is now — how can I put it . . ."

"Resurrected?" Pip suggested incredulously.

"Not exactly," Sebastian replied. "More preserved."

"Preserved!" Pip exclaimed.

"You mean like a pickled onion?" Tim went on. He looked at Pip. "Might account for the whiff."

"Do you know of embalming?" Sebastian then asked.

"The ancient Egyptians did it to their dead pharaohs," Tim replied. "I saw it on the History Channel."

"The reason for that," Sebastian explained, "was so that they could be reborn again in human form in the afterlife."

"So Scrotton's a reborn ancient Egyptian!" Pip blurted out.

"The curse of the pharaohs in the flesh?" Tim added, raising his hands, gnarling his fingers into crooked hooks and flailing his arms. "The mummy returns!"

"No," Sebastian said, "the knowledge of embalming was brought to these shores by Phoenician sailors well before the time of Our Lord Jesus. Ancient Britons learnt of it from them. Scrotton, I am certain, has never left these shores."

"So how old is he?" Tim asked.

"I would think," Sebastian answered, "he is probably the better part of 6,000 years old by now."

Pip and Tim fell silent.

"I just can't get my head around this," Tim said at length.

"Are you telling us," Pip rejoined, "that we've got a 6,000-year-old ancient British boy in our class?"

"Maybe his father worked as a brickie when they built Stonehenge," Tim ventured glibly.

"I know not what you mean by brickie," Sebastian replied, "but, yes, it is not inconceivable he was present at the construction of that megalithic monument."

"Might be an idea, sis," Tim suggested pensively, "to copy off him in history tests."

"It may well be," Sebastian agreed, "for Scrotton is not as stupid as he may seem. He is, after all, a familiar."

"A familiar what?" Tim replied.

Sebastian smiled a little indulgently. "I use the word as a noun, not as an adjective. A familiar is a companion, sometimes to an alchemist, sometimes to anyone who is involved in the magic arts."

"You mean like witches always had black cats or toads or something?" Tim suggested.

"In a manner of speaking," Sebastian agreed, "although talk of such things is more folklore than fact. A true familiar was more like a personal servant," he went on, "who catered to his master's or mistress's needs and assisted them in their work. In time, the most experienced familiars became almost as learned as those for whom they worked, for they picked up experience and knowledge along the way."

It was then that Pip and Tim remembered the words of the boy standing next to them by the lockers: *he sucks up to teachers.* This remark suddenly took on a whole new meaning — Scrotton might be Yoland's familiar. Pip, for what she thought must have been the first time in her life, felt for her brother's hand on the duvet and held it tightly.

"So," she asked quaveringly, not wanting to hear the answer, "who — or what — is Yoland?"

"You will recall," Sebastian commenced, "my speaking to you of my father who was alchemist to the court of King Henry the Fifth. When the King died, you remember how there was a power struggle to gain control and how Humfrey, Duke of Gloucester, claimed the regency of the infant King Henry the Sixth?"

Pip and Tim nodded.

"When Gloucester's plan to be regent was thwarted," Sebastian went on, "and his brother, the Duke of Bedford, was appointed regent, Gloucester set about seeking to gain power by all means. He became Protector and Defender of the Kingdom and Church and was ennobled as the Earl of Pembroke. Deeply embroiled in political activities, he needed to be able to assess what his opponents were planning. To achieve this, he needed assistance and turned to Yoland, taking him into his employ. They had first met when Yoland was a student of theology at Balliol College, in the University of Oxford."

"So Yoland was employed by Gloucester as an alchemist like your father?" Pip suggested.

"Yes!" Tim exclaimed, a sequence of events rapidly unfolding in his mind. "If he could find the way to turn iron into gold, Gloucester could have become immensely rich and raised an army and then . . ."

Sebastian held up his hand. "A fair hypothesis," he said, "but incorrect, for Yoland was not an experienced alchemist. The transmutation of metals or the fashioning of a homunculus was quite beyond his abilities. Although he possessed some alchemical knowledge from his studies, he was more of a mage, what one might call today a magician."

"A magician?" queried Tim. "You mean he pulled rabbits out of hats and eggs out of your ears?"

"No," said Sebastian with a hint of impatience at Tim's frivolity. "He was a mage, a wise man, someone who accumulated knowledge. What you describe were the actions of court entertainers and jesters."

"What sort of knowledge?" Pip asked.

Sebastian thought for a minute. "Yoland was fascinated by alchemy, as were many educated men at that time, but his real interest lay in . . ." He paused and looked out of the window towards the river, ". . . understanding the baser instincts of men. I suppose you might call him a kind of an . . ." Sebastian paused again, ". . . evil psychiatrist, a man who seeks to . . ."

". . . get inside other people's heads?" Tim suggested.

"In a manner of speaking," Sebastian responded. "His aim was to comprehend people's motivation by searching their souls. If he could understand their desires, he could manipulate their souls. In effect, steal them."

"Steal them . . . ?" Pip said.

"Not steal in the sense one might a coin or valuable object," Sebastian explained. "More to gain control over. One only has to know some of the thoughts harbored in another's soul to discover that person's innermost secrets and enter their very being. And the deeper one may go, the greater the control."

"What you really mean," Tim said, "is that once Yoland got inside the head of one of Gloucester's enemies, he could tell what it was he was after so Gloucester could give it to him and sort of buy him."

"Indeed!" Sebastian exclaimed. "And this is exactly what happened. Yet all did not go well for Gloucester. In time, he gained many enemies and his wife was imprisoned in Leeds Castle in the county of Kent, accused of sorcery. Some of his followers whom he bought, as you put it, Tim, were accused of conspiring to kill the King and put their master on the throne in his stead. Gloucester's son, Arthur, was among them."

"And after the plot was uncovered," said Pip, "all his men were executed, I suppose."

"No," Sebastian replied, "the King pardoned them. His Majesty, you see, knew of Yoland and his powers. He believed Gloucester's men and son had been bewitched."

"What happened to Gloucester?" Pip asked.

"He died in 1447," Sebastian replied. "Some believed, poisoned by followers of the Earl of Suffolk, one of his enemies. Others declared he died of palsy. Yet I heard talk and believe that Yoland killed him so that no one might discover his part in the planned overthrow of the King."

"How did Yoland kill him?" Tim inquired.

Sebastian answered, "To the best of my knowledge,

by giving him a honey and saffron quiche containing henbane."

"Quite a thought," Tim mused. "Our homeroom teacher is a murderer, a mind-bender and a traitor. They don't come worse that that! Except," he added, "maybe the Duke of Gloucester."

"Do not judge Gloucester too harshly," Sebastian responded. "He was known by many as the Good Duke Humfrey. He was a widely read and a very educated man and a great collector of books which he gave to the University of Oxford, where they remain to this day in a grand building called Duke Humfrey's Library."

"So you can go there and borrow them?" Tim asked in amazement.

Sebastian smiled. "They are not lent, being most rare, but you may enter the library and see them."

"Cool!" Tim exclaimed.

"Let me get this right," Pip said. "Yoland is able to look into people's minds, see what they are thinking and then corrupt them."

"Yes," Sebastian agreed bluntly.

"So Yoland can read minds!" Tim exclaimed. "And now he's our homeroom teacher. Cosmic!" he added ironically. "No more lame sorry-my-homework's-late-the-cat-threw-up-on-it excuses. Tell him a lie and he'll see through it. But he doesn't sound that dangerous to me. It's not as if he can turn us into newts or snails, or make another homunculus, and I see no reason why he might want to get inside our heads. We're school kids. Hardly worth bribing."

Pip listened quietly to her brother and then said,

"I'm not so sure." She looked at Sebastian. "What about his magnetizing me?"

"He was reaching out to you," Sebastian declared, "searching for you, to see how easily he might gain access to your mind."

Pip shivered at the thought and whispered, "Why me? What's in my mind that he can want? A knowledge of the best shampoo for split ends? Where to get film-star gossip on the Internet?"

"That remains to be seen," Sebastian answered, which did nothing to ease Pip's anguish.

At that moment, Mrs. Ledger called up the stairs, announcing supper.

"I shall depart," Sebastian declared, "to consider this turn of events. We shall meet again later this evening."

He opened the panel in the wall, slipping through as it closed behind him. They could hear him descending the passageway in the wall. He made less noise than a mouse in the woodwork.

"I presume you have no homework?" asked their mother as they sat down to supper.

"Not yet," said Tim. "We've not really begun any classes."

"It will come," their father predicted solemnly. "You can count on that. You'll soon forget how to operate a television remote."

After supper, Sebastian reappeared in Tim's bedroom as he sat at his computer, playing a rally driving game. For some minutes, he watched over Tim's shoulder as he swung a bright silver virtual Toyota Land Cruiser over a tortuous succession of sand dunes on the Paris–Dakar Rally. It was not until Tim reached the next checkpoint that Sebastian spoke.

"I have been considering the situation," he announced. "Let us talk."

Stopping for Pip in her room, they went downstairs and out through the kitchen. As they passed her, Mrs. Ledger said pleasantly, "Hello, Sebastian!"

"Good evening, Mrs. Ledger," he answered. "I hope you are well."

"I'm in fine spirits, thank you," she replied, smiling.

Going by the open kitchen window, Pip and Tim overheard their mother say to their father, "That Sebastian is such a polite boy. You'd hardly think he was a modern lad at all!" Pip and Tim grinned at each other and kept on walking.

Dusk was falling as they made their way over the fields towards the river, following a path Mr. Ledger had mown across the meadow. Once they reached the stand of willows that leaned out over the water, they turned and made their way along the bank in the direction of the copse of trees known since Sebastian's father's day as the Garden of Eden. Rafts of dead leaves and twigs flowed by on the current. The water was black and running fast. Tim tried to see if there were any trout in the places where the river ran over a stony bed, but his eyes were unable to penetrate the surface in the failing light.

On reaching the edge of the trees, Sebastian led the way into the cover and headed for the clearing in the middle of the copse. The beds of alchemical herbs which Pip had tidied only weeks before were now overgrown, many of the plants gone to seed or dying off. Those which were perennials were heavy with fruit or overripe berries and looked drab. In the center of the clearing stood a new oak bench which Mrs. Ledger had had placed there. She had come to love the little stand of trees, often going there on summer weekend afternoons to read or just sit with Mr. Ledger, a tray of tortilla crisps and a bottle of chilled wine or a jug of iced margarita, Mrs. Ledger's favorite summer drink, between them. Several times she had said to Pip or Tim how peaceful the clearing was, how the rest of the world hardly seemed to exist when she was there with a good book.

"It's really quite a magical place," she remarked more than once.

Her children always smiled indulgently but said nothing.

For a few minutes, Sebastian walked around the clearing, breaking off seed-heads or dead leaves and placing them in a small leather pouch hanging from his belt. When he was done, he pointed to the bench and said, "Let us be seated."

Across the river, a cock pheasant started to chirp loudly in the long grass, another taking up the call over towards the quarry. The grating sound set Pip's nerves on edge. Overhead, small birds flitted silently between the boughs as they made for their night roosts. A small breeze riffled through the branches, the leaves whispering.

"So?" Tim asked at length, breaking their silence. "What's going down, Sebastian? What's Yoland's game?"

Sebastian paused for a moment and then answered, "Whatever it is, be certain it is not a game. He shares not

Malodor's aim of creating a homunculus, for he has not the skill. He may be seeking to perfect the making of *aurum potabile*, but I do not believe this to be the case. He has no immediate need of it, for he is aging so slowly. He may, however, be concentrating on the transmutation of base metals into gold. Yet again, I think not."

"Has that ever been achieved?" Pip inquired with more than a hint of skepticism.

Sebastian smiled faintly and admitted, "There were many charlatans in my father's time who claimed success in order to gain favor with powerful men, but I saw no genuine proof. Yet," he went on, "it is possible, for science has achieved this aim in the present day. One element may indeed be transformed into another under the right conditions, with great heat and pressure. My father deduced the theory, yet the necessary conditions were unattainable in his lifetime. Today, they are."

"Yes," Tim agreed, "but not in a glass test tube in a school laboratory."

"Indeed not," Sebastian concurred. "Yet it still stands that, with the appropriate equipment, Yoland could attempt it."

"Yeah, right!" Tim exclaimed. "The appropriate equipment! A scientific research institution the size of a large town, a workforce of thousands, a budget of billions. Not exactly the tools available to a chemistry teacher following the National Curriculum. Besides," he went on, "what's the point? If you're a government, or the Bank of England or something, it might be worth your while, but as an individual, you can't do much with pure gold."

Sebastian looked puzzled. "I do not understand," he said. "Gold is most valuable."

"Time for lesson number thirty-two in twenty-first-century studies," Tim announced. "In your day, if you wanted to buy bread you took a bronze coin along to the baker and he gave you a loaf," he went on.

"Several loaves," Sebastian cut in pedantically, "and the coin was silver."

"Whatever," Tim said, searching for another example. "All right, how much would your father have paid for a good horse?"

"I know not," Sebastian replied.

"OK," said Tim, "but how did he pay for it?"

"In gold coins, usually nobles, or maybe in ounces of gold," Sebastian declared. "It was the way."

"Exactly," said Tim. "Today, it's different. Sure, if you want to buy something you could still use a coin." He took a pound coin out of his pocket, spun it in midair, caught it and put it back in his pocket. "It looks like gold, but it's not a gold coin at all. And it's not worth that much either. Enough for a bag of fries if you're lucky. What we can't do is go to a bank and withdraw or deposit gold. Walk up to the counter and try to pay in a gold and, bingo! The alarms go off, the bars go down, the doors lock and you'll be surrounded by the Old Bill in seconds."

"Old Bill who?" Sebastian asked.

"It's a nickname for the police," Pip explained.

"My point is," Tim said, "even if Yoland had the means, making gold would be a waste of time as he couldn't spend it or convert it into cash without raising suspicion. You can't sell gold unless it's already been made into something, like jewelry, and you can't buy gold, jewelry apart, unless you're a licensed gold dealer. All our money these days is really virtual money. He'd do better magically counterfeiting credit cards or debit cards."

"Debit cards?" Sebastian echoed.

Tim took his wallet out of his hip pocket and slid his Switch card free of the leather. "This," he held it out to Sebastian, "is a computer-coded slip of plastic which, when run through a card reader in a shop, can debit money from my savings account in the bank on the spot. I buy something but no actual money changes hands."

Sebastian took the card, turning it over and closely scrutinizing it.

"This is indeed a fascinating concept," he declared.

From the far end of the Garden of Eden came the soft hoot of a tawny owl. Sebastian looked up, searching the trees to locate the bird.

"Is the owl . . . ?" Pip began.

"There is no cause for alarm," Sebastian quickly reassured her. "We are secure here. The owl is but an owl."

The bird took to the wing, flying slowly through the trees towards them. It settled on a bough of a sycamore, sending a small shower of helicopter-winged seeds pirouetting to the ground.

"I believe," Sebastian said finally, "you are correct, Tim. He is not trying to transmute metals for he has not the ability. Once, he tried to gain my father's assistance in this but my father, realizing Yoland was dishonorable, refused to assist him, and his efforts came to nothing."

"So Yoland, like Malodor, was your father's enemy," Pip said.

"Yoland," Sebastian replied softly, "was one of those who betrayed my father. He was one of those," he went on, "who put firebrands to my father's pyre."

Tim put a consoling hand on Sebastian's shoulder.

The owl took to the wing once more, flying across the river and off into the gathering night. Pip watched its ungainly flight until it disappeared in the dusk.

"Night falls and we must return," Sebastian declared. "It is in the hours of darkness that evil thrives."

They stood up and began the walk across the field towards the house. Far off, a small flock of two dozen sheep clustered together under a spreading oak. They belonged to Geoff, a local farmer to whom Mr. Ledger gave the grazing rights. In what little daylight was left, they looked like clumps of dense mist hugging the ground. As the three of them drew near, a few of the animals rose to their feet, their rear quarters rising clumsily before their front. Tim, who was carrying his halogen flashlight, shone it on the sheep's faces. As the beam caught their eyes they reflected a brilliant silver.

"Look!" he joked. "They've got their headlights on."

The first period of the following morning's time-table was biology. The teacher, a young woman called Miss Bates, was clearly passionate about her subject and eager to enthuse her pupils.

"Biology," she announced, "is the study of life, of living organisms smaller than a pinhead or bigger than an elephant." To illustrate her point, she had set up a row of microscopes and specimens down one side of her laboratory. One by one the class took turns to study them. Pip was entranced by some minuscule creatures cavorting in half a centimeter of water in a flat Petri dish. According to a label next to them, they were *Daphnia pulex*, the common water flea. When Tim asked if they bit like dog or cat fleas, Miss Bates smiled and assured him that they did not. The next specimen was a prepared glass slide containing a butterfly's wing, the scales iridescent under the light shining upon it. Next to that was a cross-section of a plant stem showing the various vessels carrying sap.

As everyone made their way around this display, Tim happened to catch sight of Scrotton. He was not following everyone else but keeping close to the teacher, asking her specific questions about the specimens. She, Tim noticed, answered them but it was obvious she was annoyed by Scrotton and, eventually, she asked him to return to his seat. He obeyed but Tim saw him scowl behind her back.

When the tour of specimens was over, Miss Bates ordered each pupil to return to one of them and draw what they saw on the first page of their biology notebooks. Tim chose a cow's tooth that had been vertically sawn in half, showing the root, nerve canal and layers of enamel and dentin. Pip decided to attempt a water flea, accepted it was too great a task and concentrated instead on the butterfly wing, drawing as accurately as she could the veins and feathering on the edge.

Towards the end of the lesson, Pip happened to pause and sit upright to ease her muscles. Sitting on a stool at a laboratory bench, bending forward to concentrate on the microscope and her drawing, had made her back ache. As she stretched her shoulders, she happened to look up at the rows of preserved specimens on shelves at the side of the room. In one large sealed jar, a dissected frog was spread-eagled against a sheet of Perspex, held in place by threads at the ends of its limbs. Its intestines had been removed to show its blood system, the veins and arteries stained different colors. From each organ stretched a thin white cord terminating in a plastic label identifying it.

"A chamber of horrors," Tim remarked quietly. "Biology might be the study of life but apart from that potted cactus," he glanced in the direction of the laboratory window, "those water fleas, Miss Bates and us, everything else in here's met a grisly end."

Yet, no sooner had he spoken than Pip flinched.

"What's up, sis?" Tim inquired.

Nodding in the direction of the specimen display shelf, she muttered, "That frog . . ."

"What about it, sis?"

"It's . . ." Pip began.

"It's what?"

". . . alive."

"That's crazy!" Tim retorted. "A zombie frog."

Pip was certain the frog was returning to life. Its heart was feebly pulsing, its limbs, pinioned to the transparent sheet, were flexing as if the creature was struggling to break free. Its head moved from side to side.

"It is!" Pip rejoined sharply.

"No way!" Tim replied, staring up at the specimen

jar. "That one's definitely hopped its last hop. You'll be telling me next one of the pickled eyes winked at you."

"Look at it!" Pip insisted.

To humor his sister, Tim did so. The frog, the flesh of which was blanched by years of immersion in formaldehyde preserving liquid, was irremovably transfixed to the Perspex.

"There!" Pip muttered urgently. She was sure the frog's hind leg jerked, kicking out at one of the label cords. "See it?"

"No," Tim answered. "Not a flicker. I tell you, sis, it's croaked its last croak."

What neither of them noticed was Scrotton watching them from behind an exercise book, grinning.

That evening, as Pip sat on her bed watching television, the panel in the wall opened and Sebastian stepped into the room.

"You could learn to knock, too," she commented caustically.

"Please accept my apology," Sebastian answered. "It is not my intention to catch you unawares. It is that I am not accustomed to finding the house occupied, even after the several months of your living here. For many years, the house has been unoccupied over long periods, and I have grown used to being the only resident." He sat on Pip's dressing-table stool, facing her.

"What about the old man who lived here? Your so-called uncle?"

"He was not here for long," Sebastian replied evasively.

"After your father's death," Pip continued, "why didn't his enemies take over the house? They must have wanted it."

"Indeed, they did," Sebastian agreed, "yet they dared not."

"Why not?"

"Because they were afraid," Sebastian answered bluntly.

"Afraid of what?" Pip came back.

"Afraid of me," Sebastian said.

Pip stared at him.

"Of you?"

"Of what I can do," Sebastian answered.

Tim, hearing them speaking, came in from his room, dumping himself down on the end of Pip's bed.

"Anyone invited to this party?" He grinned at Pip and winked. "Or am I the spare sandwich at the picnic?"

Pip gave her brother a look she hoped might silence him for the rest of the evening. Or longer. For his part, Tim mimed zipping his mouth shut.

"I have," Sebastian stated, "today given much thought to Yoland."

"So what do you reckon he's up to?" Tim asked.

"That I cannot surmise," Sebastian admitted, "and in order to discover more, I feel I need to enter your school, to observe him for myself."

"Neat!" Tim exclaimed, remembering his walk during the summer with Sebastian on a lead, disguised as a brown-and-white Jack Russell terrier. "What will you go as? You can't go in as a JRT. Not into classrooms, anyway."

"He could go in as a pet mouse," Pip suggested. "There's a girl in my gym group who has a pet rat she keeps in her pocket. It lives in a box in her locker during PE."

"How about a cat?" Tim suggested. "I've seen one wandering about."

"I need wider access than is afforded to an animal," Sebastian said, "for I cannot see Yoland permitting such a creature in his laboratory. Besides, I need more than to observe him in passing. I must study him, get close to him. To this end," he declared, "I need to join your class."

Tim and Pip exchanged a glance.

"That's not going to be easy," Pip declared. "You can't just walk into the school. You're going to have to get registered, be entered on the database."

"That's not all," Tim said. "You're going to have to have a uniform. And you don't just need to look like us. You'll need to be like us. We'll have to make you into a modern kid."

Sebastian looked somewhat hurt and rejoined, "I do not see that I am dissimilar to you."

Tim laughed. "You must be joking!"

"I jest not!" Sebastian exclaimed.

"I jest not!" Tim repeated and he looked at Pip. "We've got a serious makeover to do here and it's going to take a lot more than a school jacket and a pair of sneakers."

Sebastian looked himself up and down and replied, somewhat ironically, "I do not see that modern boys have three arms or five legs. Since I was born, I do not see that human anatomy has changed very much."

"No," Tim agreed, "it hasn't, but just about everything else has."

"Very well," said Sebastian, standing stiffly in the middle of the room as if waiting for a tailor to fit him with a suit, "teach me to be modern."

Pip and Tim ran their eyes over Sebastian. "Well," Pip said eventually, switching off her television, "let's get on with it."

"For a start," Tim began, "you've got to chill out."

"Chill out?" Sebastian looked somewhat puzzled.

"Be relaxed," Tim explained. "Let it all hang out."

"Let what hang out?" Sebastian asked. "Hang out of what?"

"It's an expression," Pip said.

"Don't be so uptight all the time," Tim went on. "Life's less formal now. For example, language isn't so exact. Don't say 'Good morning,' say 'Morning' or 'How're you doing?' or just 'Hi.' Don't say 'I do not like that,' say 'That's uncool.' If you like something, say 'That's really cool.'"

"A state of low temperature seems to have become a superlative," Sebastian remarked sardonically.

For half an hour, Pip and Tim attempted to tutor Sebastian in modern slang. For his part, Sebastian found it difficult to understand why a "mare" meant awful, while a "piece of cake" meant easy. He could not see the connection between, as he put it, the female of a horse or a pastry and a state of unattractiveness or ease of function. Nor could he comprehend why a simple meal of bread and sausage should be called a "hot dog." "Knackered" he did grasp, for there had been knackers in the fifteenth century, but how the noun for a horse slaughterer had come to mean the verb "to be tired" was a linguistic leap he could not rationalize. As for what a "blockbuster" was, Sebastian was totally lost.

"Look," Tim said at length, "don't try and work out how these words came about. Just accept that they have."

"Finally," said Pip, "there's the word 'wicked.'"

"Of that," Sebastian declared, "I think I am more than acquainted with the meaning."

"It means super, superlative," Pip said.

"Like," Tim explained, "someone has a state of the art, brand new, multi-gear mountain bike . . ."

". . . and you say," Pip stated, "'That bike's wicked.'" Sebastian stared at them.

"I fail totally to comprehend . . ." he began.

"Don't try," Tim said. "Just accept it."

"And," Pip advised, "when we go to school, if you're having problems just keep your mouth shut, listen and learn. Be polite to the teachers, but let the rest of us do the talking. You'll soon catch on."

"Catch on?" Sebastian repeated.

Tim looked to the ceiling and said, "Yes, get the drift, pick it up, go with the flow. Whatever you do, don't say 'I wonder if we will experience inclement weather today' when what you mean is it looks like rain. People will wonder what planet you've fallen off."

"One cannot fall off a planet," Sebastian answered. "The gravitational forces . . ."

"Enough!" Tim exclaimed, holding up his hand.

"Getting the lingo right's one thing," said Pip, "but . . . Well, look at the way you stand."

"I see nothing wrong with my stance," Sebastian defended himself.

"You look as if you're on parade," Tim said. "Nobody stands up straight these days. We all slouch."

"Yes," said Sebastian with more than a hint of disparagement, "I've noticed."

"And we don't dress neatly either. We look reasonable in our school uniforms," Pip said, "but it's a uniform, it's not exactly what we'd wear if we wanted to. So, you know, sometimes you let your shirt hang out a bit or let your tie loose. You probably have to tuck them in or tighten them up when the teachers come, but the rest of the time you don't. You just . . ."

"Hang it all loose?" suggested Sebastian.

Tim laughed. "Not exactly. Hanging loose is what we do. What your clothes do is just stick out over your belt."

"Life in this century," said Sebastian, "is indeed more relaxed than in that of my father's time, but you must remember that then I lived in royal circles where people dressed smartly and manners and courtly behavior were important. Yet I would add that not all of England was like that. The peasantry wore very crude and rough clothing, did not adhere to a life of manners and were far more like the people of today."

"Are you implying," Tim said, feigning anger, "that we are all peasants?"

Sebastian looked at Tim, replying indirectly, "You are as you would choose to regard yourself."

While they had been talking, Pip had been studying Sebastian.

"There's something else as well," she decided and, stepping across to Sebastian, stood by his side. "You'll have to excuse me, but . . ." Reaching up, she ran her fingers through his hair, tousling it. No sooner had her fingers left it, however, than it fell back into its former shape.

Sebastian's hairstyle was certainly not that of a modern boy. It was too long, and it curled under slightly. It reminded Pip of pageboys in history books.

"We've got to do something about this," Pip announced. "There's only one thing to do."

She fumbled in a drawer of her dressing table and took out a pair of long-bladed scissors. Four minutes later, Sebastian had a new haircut, short behind his ears but a little bit longer at the back. In places, odd strands stuck out.

"I might be able to sort that out with a bit of gel," said Pip and she held up a mirror for Sebastian. "There you are — welcome to the twenty-first century."

Sebastian studied himself in the mirror.

"What do you think?" asked Tim.

"Well, to be quite truthful," Sebastian answered, "I am not unduly impressed."

"I think," Tim said to his sister, "that means he doesn't like it."

At breakfast the following day, Tim was very pensive. Usually chatty with his parents, he seemed deep in thought. Pip knew what he was thinking, for she too had the same concerns. It was one thing to cut Sebastian's hair and teach him to either keep his mouth closed or speak slightly more modern English, but quite another to get him a uniform and enter his details onto the school server.

For most of the morning, Tim pondered the problem. The only computers he saw were those in the school secretary's office or the IT classroom. At the mid-morning break, he sauntered into a joining-up meeting for the computer club, solely in the hope that it might give him access to the IT computers. It did: but they were not connected to the school intranet.

"We're out of luck," he told Pip as the bell rang, but, in the period after break, he saw his chance.

A library prefect came around the school to take all new pupils for a library orientation session.

Just inside the main library door was a large wooden desk behind which sat the librarian. As the pupils entered, they lined up at the desk and were issued library cards, the information entered into the computer. Tim watched as the librarian logged on, typing in her user name and password. It was simplicity itself – her name, according to a badge she wore pinned to her sweater, was Mrs. Anne Patterson. Her user name was *pata*. Her password, Tim saw as she typed it, was *books*.

Waiting until everyone had been issued with their library cards, Tim murmured to Pip, "Distract her. Get her away from the desk."

Pip nodded.

A few minutes later, she went across to the desk and said, "Excuse me, miss. Could you please explain the classification system to me? We didn't have anything like this in our junior school."

"Well, certainly," said the librarian, evidently surprised that here was a child actually asking to be shown around the library rather than taking it for granted and later mixing up all the books on the shelves. "Come with me and I'll show you how it works."

The librarian stepped out from behind her desk. Tim waited until she and Pip were out of sight around the end of the first row of shelves then, checking that he was unobserved, he slid behind the desk and quickly punched in the woman's access details. Immediately, he was into the school server.

As quickly as he could, he made a new entry in the registration file. For Sebastian's Christian name he entered *Sebastian*, thinking the less complicated he made things the better; for his surname he put down *Gillette*, the name of the razor his father used. Where the software requested a previous junior school address, Tim invented one off the top of his head and located it in Manchester, as far away and in the biggest city he could think of on the spur of the moment. As for Sebastian's home address, he typed in *The Cottage, Rawne Barton*, grinning as he did so. After all, he thought, Sebastian did have an entry to his underground laboratory there and the building, the old coach house which was going to be converted into an office for his father, was a genuine postal address. He typed in Sebastian's parents as being Mr. David and Mrs. Anna Gillette.

No sooner had he pressed *return* and logged off than the librarian and Pip reappeared. Pip gave Tim a quick look to make sure he was finished. He gave her a sly nod and walked out.

Sitting together eating their sandwiches in the dining hall at lunchtime, Tim said in an undertone, "He's Gillette, Sebastian, and he's in our homeroom."

At the end of the day, as they were about to leave the school, Pip said, "Only one obstacle to go now. Gillette, S. needs a school uniform."

"No problemo!" Tim remarked. "Just stand outside that door and keep your bag open."

Pip did as she was told. Tim opened the swing door and disappeared through into the boys' locker room. Beyond, in the gymnasium, two soccer teams were warming up. Tim quickly worked his way along the row of hooks, looking for a jacket and a pair of pants that might fit Sebastian. It was not a difficult task, for Sebastian was more or less his size and Tim did not have to search for long. In under thirty seconds, he had them bundled under his arm. Walking as nonchalantly as he could towards the door, he stepped outside, checked that the corridor was empty and dumped them in Pip's bag. She rapidly zipped it up.

"I feel really guilty," Pip admitted.

Tim smirked and said, "All for a good cause."

It was only as they set off down the corridor that Tim realized he had forgotten something.

"Hold on," he said. "Got to go back." He disappeared into the locker room again, to reappear with a school tie scrunched up in his hand.

"Cinch!" he exclaimed to Pip, and they left the building.

That evening, in Tim's bedroom, Sebastian put on his school uniform with a pair of Tim's sneakers and one of his shirts. As he dressed, Tim collected together some ballpoint pens, pencils, an eraser and a ruler as well as an old calculator, put them in a tattered pencil case he had used in primary school and placed that in an airline bag he had picked up on vacation two years before.

"Very sharp," Pip said sarcastically when Sebastian was dressed. "You look like one of us."

"Really?" Tim replied.

"Well, almost," Pip said.

"He is what he is," Tim retorted. "A fifteenth-century imitation of a twenty-first-century kid."

"Certainly with the haircut," Sebastian ruefully agreed. "Yet I shall do my best to conform to your standards."

Tim shrugged.

"There is one thing," said Pip. "We'd better cut out the name tag of the boy whose jacket and pants we stole."

She took the clothes and removed the owner's name tags with a pair of nail scissors, replacing them with some of Tim's.

"That won't just fool the school," Pip said, "but Mum as well. It means we can put Master Gillette's laundry in with ours."

"I have been considering another quandary," Sebastian remarked. "How do I get to the school? It is some distance."

"Can't you sort of use magic to make your way there?" Tim suggested. "Turn up as a bird and change into human mode in a stall in the boys' room or behind the bike sheds."

"Yes," Sebastian agreed, "that is possible but not wise. When I arrive, it must seem as if I am doing so in the fashion of my peers. Yoland and Scrotton will be watching. A boy appearing suddenly around the end of a building he had not already stepped behind might arouse suspicion."

"We'll have to give him a lift," said Pip.

"Mum'll pull up at the side of the road if she sees him," Tim stated. "She thinks the sun shines out of his earhole. What I suggest you do, Sebastian, is stand on the first corner of the road after the Rawne Barton turn-off. Our mother will have to slow down there to take the bend. Just put yourself where she can see you and keep walking slowly as if you're on your way to school."

"Very well," said Sebastian, "but what do you mean by your remark concerning the sun?"

"Let it go," Tim replied, grinning. "It's just an expression. Take it as a compliment."

Sebastian shrugged, shook his head and said, "I will bid you goodnight and shall see you on the morrow at the aforementioned location."

"Try that again," Tim requested.

Sebastian thought for a moment and then replied, "Goodnight. I'll see you in the morning at the place upon which we have agreed."

"Better," Tim said. "Not perfect, but definitely better."

With that, Sebastian stepped through the panel in the wall and disappeared.

"Think we can pull this off?" Pip asked as the faint sounds of Sebastian's descent down the hidden passage receded.

"Do you?" Tim replied.

"It's going to be a long haul," she answered. "Getting him on the school register and making him look like Joe Bloggs in Year Seven was a cinch compared to what's coming."

"Tell me about it," Tim replied. "If we get a 'quandary' or two and a couple of 'See you on the morrows' on the morrow, we'll be in for it."

The following morning, as arranged, they came upon Sebastian walking along the side of the road as Mrs. Ledger slowed for the corner.

"Is that Sebastian?" she remarked.

"Yes, it is!" Tim replied, feigning surprise. "Do you think we can give him a lift?"

"Of course," said Mrs. Ledger. "If we don't he'll be very late." She paused. "How does he usually get to school?"

"He walks, I think," said Tim.

"Walks!" exclaimed Mrs. Ledger. "It's over six miles!"

"Well, maybe he walks to the crossroads and catches the bus," Tim added.

"Maybe he's got a bicycle," suggested Pip.

"Well, he hasn't got it now," their mother answered. She pulled in to the side of the road and leaned across to open the front passenger door.

"Good morning, Mrs. Ledger," Sebastian said politely.

"Good morning, Sebastian," she greeted him. "Would you like a lift?"

"Yes, thank you very much," he replied.

Sebastian got in the front seat.

"Seat belt," Mrs. Ledger said as she put the car in gear.

Sebastian looked a little confused and glanced at Pip. Sitting in the back, she tugged at her seat belt and pretended to pull it across herself to the buckle. Sebastian got the message and buckled up.

"The first of many faux pas . . ." Tim muttered to his sister.

Mrs. Ledger concentrated on her driving. None of them spoke very much during the journey to the school and, on arrival at the gates, they joined the throng of other pupils arriving by parent's car, bicycle, school bus, or on foot. Half a dozen teachers stood around in the playground watching the arrivals, prefects guiding those new pupils with bicycles towards the cycle racks. Pip and Tim headed for their classroom, followed by Sebastian. They noticed how Sebastian looked around all the time, not so much out of curiosity, but fleetingly scrutinizing the faces of the other pupils and teachers.

Reaching the corridor near the chemistry laboratory, Tim opened his locker, telling Sebastian the combination to the padlock. This done, the three of them entered the laboratory.

Yoland was standing behind the demonstration bench, engrossed in setting up equipment for a senior-school experiment. He only looked up briefly to acknowledge their entrance. Sebastian walked right around the outer walls of the room, glancing from cupboard to cupboard, studying the bottles of reagents and acids, the jars and tins of chemicals behind the glass doors. He then came and sat next to Pip and Tim at the end of one of the benches.

"Do you see anything?" whispered Tim.

"I see many things," said Sebastian enigmatically.

"I think what Tim meant was," murmured Pip, "do you see anything interesting?"

"Oh, yes," Sebastian went on obtusely, his voice disguised by the sound of pupils talking and laughing in the corridor. "I see much of interest every day when I am abroad in your era."

Gradually, the room filled. The pupils sat on the stools at the benches, arranging their books for the morning's lessons, taking out their pens, a few of them switching off their mobile phones. The last person to enter the room was Scrotton.

"Good morning," Yoland said loudly, his voice silencing the pupils' hubbub. "I've mentioned to you already a few basic rules to be observed in here. I will now elaborate upon these. Pay particular attention. Do not put your food on the benches. Do not lick your pencils or your pens. Many of the substances in here are poisonous and are sometimes spilled on the benches. Keep your hands washed. Move around the room slowly and with caution. Just a swing of your coat pocket or a nudge of your elbow can be dangerous. Whenever I come in the room, you fall silent. This is not just out of manners and due deference to me as your teacher but, more importantly, so that you hear instructions."

As Yoland spoke, Sebastian continued to study the contents of the cabinets, taking in all the equipment and considering how it might be used. There was much with which he was not familiar.

Suddenly, Yoland stopped talking and, pointing at Sebastian, said, "You!"

Sebastian looked up. "Yes, sir?"

"What do you think you're doing, boy? Pay attention."

"Yes, sir," replied Sebastian.

Yoland looked at him closely for a moment. Tim's heart missed a beat. Pip felt the skin of her brow tighten with fear. They were both thinking the same thing: *had Yoland recognized Sebastian?*

"You haven't been here before," the teacher remarked.

"No, sir," said Sebastian, "I arrived late."

"Did you indeed," said Yoland. "I do not like late pupils any more than I do inattentive ones." He opened the class register. "Name?"

"Sebastian Gillette, sir."

The teacher turned to Scrotton. "Go to the office and ask the secretary for Gillette's entry slip."

Scrotton disappeared to return a few minutes later with a computer printout. Yoland studied it and entered the details in the register, commenting as he did so, "I had no idea there was a cottage at Rawne Barton."

"It was the coach house, sir," said Tim, jumping in to help Sebastian out of difficulty. "It's being converted, sir, into an office for my father and a vacation home. We've rented it to the Gillettes for the winter, sir. They're renting it while they look for a house to buy."

"Are they now?" Yoland responded with a feigned lack of interest.

He took the register and the bell rang for first period.

As they made their way towards the math department, Tim sighed with relief and said, "Good guys
one, Yoland nil."

"I thought for a moment he had recognized you,"
Pip said.

"He will not," Sebastian replied. "He and I were
never formally introduced in my father's time. I was but
a boy. Likewise Scrotton. I have previously seen him
from afar but he knows me not. Yet," Sebastian added,
"we must beware, for they are assuredly in league and,
together, may be a potent force with which to reckon."

Three

The Suggestion of Chimerae

The first biology homework they were given was to find, identify, and draw a living creature of their own choice which they had to obtain from the wild. Tim decided on a woodlouse, not only because they were plentiful around the firewood stack behind the coach house but also because a woodlouse was simplicity itself to draw. Sebastian and Pip, however, were more ambitious. Sebastian decided to concentrate on an earthworm while Pip, having been captivated by the water fleas, decided to search for other minute water-dwelling creatures.

"You'll need to look in permanent water," Tim declared. "What about the Roman pond? It doesn't come more permanent than 2,000 years old."

Pip cast her mind back to the summer when Sebastian had waded in the dark water and duckweed, feeling with his toes to find a silver Roman coin from the mud, cast in there as an offering to the gods sometime in the third century.

Putting on her Wellington boots and carrying a red plastic bucket, Pip set off in the direction of the spring, crossing Rawne's Ground, the largest of the fields. With autumn approaching, the grass was short and tussocky, eaten down by the sheep which now stood in a huddle against a far hedge, watching her as she made her way to the pond. The soil around it had been paddled into a slick black cloying quagmire by the sheep's hooves.

Pip dipped the bucket into the water, letting it fill to the quarter mark.

Across the field, the sheep started to amble towards her. Pip ignored them. Whenever she had come into the field, the sheep had always come up to her, their eyes vacantly watching her with the vague, blank expression of their species. Even the elderly ram, who had only one short stub of a horn, had paid her little attention.

The edge of the pool, where the feeder spring bubbled to the surface, was surrounded on three sides by a low curbing of cut stone, the water running off through a stone-lined channel at the other end. During the summer, when the grass was long, the stones had been hidden, but now they were to be plainly seen, fitting perfectly together without any mortar.

It was, Pip considered, incredible to think that Roman soldiers had stood on these very stones. Reaching down, she tugged a clump of sedge free of the mud, adding the plant to the bucket in the hope the roots might be teeming with minute life. She knew most of whatever she found would, like the *Daphnia*, be too small to draw without a microscope, but she did have a powerful magnifying glass and hoped that might suffice for water bugs that could be seen by the naked eye.

As the roots broke the surface, Pip caught sight of something dull red in the mud. Bending, she picked it up, rubbing it clean in the water. It was a piece of pottery decorated with the outline of an animal. She studied it closely. The creature appeared to be some fabled beast with a tooth-lined jaw, the rounded ears of a rat and an almost feline tail. It was running. In front of it, where the pottery had broken, severing it, were the hindquarters of another creature in full flight, its hind legs stretched out.

She placed the pottery shard in her pocket and stepped out of the pool. A large bubble of rank-smelling gas broke the surface of the water where the mud was pulling at her boot.

"Devil farting!" exclaimed Tim with a grin.

Pip jumped, struggling to keep her balance, her boots splashing.

"You don't knock, you creep up on people. After what we've been through this summer . . . it's not funny. Anyway," she added, "what're you doing out here?"

"The woodlouse is boring," Tim admitted. "I came to see if there were any newts in the pond. Now you've muddied it up with your stomping about, my chances of catching one are ten percent less than nil. Let's head back and get drawing." He nodded at the bucket. "There must be something in all the gloop."

As they turned away from the spring, another, larger bubble of gas erupted from where the water was rising. It drifted slowly to the surface, floated for a moment on the current, and then burst. The gas inside ignited with a brief, faint green flame that danced over the water before fading into thin air.

Pip leaped back, almost dropping the bucket.

"What was that?" she said, her voice high-pitched with fear.

"Marsh gas," Tim replied nonchalantly. "Made by rotting vegetation. It can ignite itself. They call it will-o'-the-wisp. Don't be so uptight. It's nothing to fret about."

Pip was unconvinced. "I thought marsh gas was methane," she answered.

"It is," Tim confirmed.

"Well," Pip replied. "Methane burns with a blue flame. Anyone with a natural gas cooker knows."

"Trick of the light," Tim answered. "If you're so worried, look at the pendant."

Pip looked down inside her T-shirt. The crystal was as clear as a shard of window glass. She touched it. It shivered violently.

"Run!" she yelled and, dropping the bucket, took to her heels. Tim followed. The sheep, seeing them in flight, broke into an easy lope behind them.

They had gone halfway to the field gate near the house when Tim called out breathlessly, "Hang on a minute, sis! My legs weren't made for running in Wellies. Anyway, what're we running from?"

He glanced back over his shoulder. The sheep were still following but were some fifty meters away and little more than sauntering along in their usual clumsy manner, like mopheads with legs.

"I don't know," Pip replied. "The pendant went clear."

"That was by the pool," Tim answered. "What is it now?"

Taking a quick look, Pip said, "Going cloudy."

"And vibrating?" Tim asked.

"No," Pip replied.

"Then we're safe," Tim declared, and he slowed to a jog.

Breathing heavily, her lungs aching, Pip also slowed to a walk, casting a cautious look behind her as she did so. The sheep were following them at a steady pace, the ram leading the flock. As she looked at it, it bleated once, loudly. In its open mouth, she saw the sharp, pointed canines of a predator. From one of its canine fangs hung strands of tattered, bloody flesh. The wool along the side of the ram's head and its muzzle were matted with gore as if it had just had its head sunk deep in the carcass of its last kill.

Pip accelerated to a sprint, Tim at her side. Her feet snagged on tussocks of grass, slipping where the sheep had cropped the field short. Her legs ached with the effort of wearing the heavy boots. At every step the rubber struck her shins, chafing the skin raw.

Reaching the field gate, Pip hurled herself at it, climbing the five wooden bars with a speed she did not know she possessed. Tim vaulted it in one, his left boot flying off into the air. Landing on the far side, they stood next to each other, gasping. Pip felt her knees weaken. The sheep trotted up to the gate and stood in a jumble.

"They're just sheep," Tim said, staring at them shamefacedly. "What were we running for?"

"Look at their teeth," Pip said, but no sooner had she spoken than the ram bleated again, one of the ewes responding to him. Their teeth were the normal, flat incisors and worn molars of grazing animals, their heads clean of anything but a few bramble twigs ensnared in the wool.

"Guess you'll have to do a woodlouse, too," Tim remarked, adding, "or a snail." He pulled his Wellington boot back on. "There's one on the gatepost."

"Who's going back for Mum's bucket?" Pip wondered aloud, looking hopefully at Tim.

"All right, I'll get it," Tim replied wearily. "A few lamb chops on the hoof don't spook me." He waved his hand at the sheep. "Mint sauce," Tim shouted derisively as they trundled off over the field.

Just before six o'clock that evening, Sebastian appeared in Tim's bedroom, still wearing his school uniform.

"I see you are addressing the extramural task set by Miss Bates," he remarked, glancing over Tim's shoulder as he drew the outline of the woodlouse on his sketch pad, the picture appearing on his computer screen.

"I presume you mean," Tim said sharply, "doing your homework? Really, Sebastian. You've got to make an effort with the lingo."

"Your computer," Sebastian replied, ignoring Tim's criticism, "is truly a remarkable example of human inventiveness and ingenuity."

"It's cool," Tim answered bluntly, giving Sebastian a pointed look.

Sebastian smiled and said, "When needs must, I shall adopt the modern idiom. However, to use such lackadaisical language all the while seems alien and gauche to me."

"Well," Tim came back at him, "that was quite a mouthful."

Beneath the drawing, he added the words: *Woodlouse, a land-dwelling crustacean, order Isopoda, class Malacostraca,* saved his drawing to the hard disk and printed it out.

"In my father's time," Sebastian said as the printer ejected the sheet of paper, "the woodlouse was known as the sow-bug or pill-bug. A powder of desiccated sow-bugs taken with warm milk was considered most beneficial in instances of stomachache or constipation."

"You've got to be kidding!" Tim exclaimed, aghast. "You mean you ate them?"

"Medicinally, yes," Sebastian answered. "Or they were made into a salve or ointment, although I forget their curative properties when applied thus."

"Never mind the lesson in medieval medicine," Pip said, entering the room with a drawing of a large snail which she slipped into Tim's scanner. "Have you told Sebastian what happened this afternoon?"

"The sheep in the field scared the daylights out of Pip," Tim replied.

"That's not fair," Pip retorted. "It wasn't like that at all. We went to the Roman pool to collect some water and bugs."

"Marsh gas bubbled out of the mud," Tim went on, "and ignited."

"*Ignis fatuus,*" Sebastian said. "The fire of fools. It has misguided many unwary travelers into mires and quicksand, they who have followed its blue light assuming it to be a distant habitation."

"Show us what you found," Tim suggested.

Pip took the shard out of her pocket and handed it to Sebastian.

"The gas burned green," Pip butted in.

"This is Roman," Sebastian declared, "a fragment of what is known as Samian ware. It was made in Gaul, which you now call France." He held it under Tim's reading lamp.

"The marsh gas burned green," Pip repeated, her exasperation growing.

"What is it?" Tim asked.

"It bears a depiction of the chimera," Sebastian said, "a Greek mythological monster with the head of a lion, the body of a goat and the ability to breathe fire."

Pip was beginning to lose patience and said, "Excuse me, can we leave the archaeology lecture and get back to the here and now? The point is that, by the pool, the pendant went clear as window glass. The marsh gas burned green and, although it was lost on my computer-nerd sibling here, the sheep had the teeth of a tiger and . . ." She fell silent as the implication of what she had just said dawned on her.

"I saw the chimera," she half whispered. "Didn't I?"

There came a knock on Tim's bedroom door and Mrs. Ledger looked in. "Supper time," she announced then, seeing Sebastian, added, "Would you like to join us, Sebastian?"

"Yes, thank you," Sebastian replied, smiling politely.

"I see you've had your hair cut," Mrs. Ledger observed. "Quite a change, if you don't mind my saying so."

The moment she had gone, Sebastian's smile vanished. "You say the marsh gas burned with a *green* flame?"

"Yes," Pip confirmed. "As green as . . ."

It was then she remembered the ancient lantern Malodor had used, its flame burning the color of weak emerald.

"And did this noxious gas reach your nostrils?"

Pip nodded apprehensively.

"In that case," Sebastian continued, "it explains your vision of the sheep. They were not, as it were, wolves in sheep's clothing and truly carnivorous, but a projection of your fears," he explained. "You saw what, at that moment, you most feared, albeit you knew it not."

"You mean they were just a figment of my imagination?" Pip asked.

"Not exactly," Sebastian replied. "More a figment of your imagination after it had been manipulated."

Pip stopped on the landing, her hand on the wall to steady herself.

"Manipulated!" she exclaimed. "What do you mean?"

"Influenced," Sebastian replied curtly.

"How?" Pip asked, in a tremulous voice.

"Perhaps by the marsh gas."

"Perhaps!" Pip repeated. "You mean you don't know?"

Sebastian did not respond.

"It's not Malodor returning?" Pip half whispered.

Still, Sebastian did not answer but, as they descended the stairs, he advised, "Do not approach the pool unless I accompany you."

"Bet your boots we won't!" Tim replied.

To this, Sebastian responded, "Why should I wager my footwear?"

Three plates of poached eggs, baked beans, chips and crisp slices of bacon were already on the kitchen table when they sat down. Sebastian looked at the beans and prodded them tentatively with his fork. Mrs. Ledger watched him.

"Don't you like baked beans, Sebastian?" she asked.

"Yes," Sebastian replied as Tim nudged his ankle under the table with his foot. "I find them to be most . . ." Tim kicked harder. "They're very nice."

Mrs. Ledger sat down opposite them with a cup of tea.

"Tell me, Sebastian," she said, "what's your surname?"

"Gillette," said Tim.

"I'm sure Sebastian's got a tongue of his own, Tim," Mrs. Ledger remarked tersely. "And where exactly do you live now, Sebastian? I know you once lived here."

"At Pleasance Farm," Sebastian replied, "the other side of Foxhanger Hill. I live there with my mother's cousin."

Tim and Pip exchanged a glance. They had suspected there might have been an ulterior motive to the invitation to supper but had not expected as thorough a grilling as the bacon slices had received.

"Does your relative own the farm?"

"No, Mrs. Ledger," Sebastian went on, "my mother's cousin's husband is the rancher."

"Your family must be long established in the area," Mrs. Ledger remarked.

"In a manner of speaking," Sebastian answered.

Pip and Tim looked at each other: six hundred years could make Sebastian's a local family.

"And do you have any brothers or sisters?"

"I am an only child," Sebastian announced.

He watched Pip as she cut off a piece of the crisp

bacon, speared it on her fork and dipped it in the poached egg yolk. It was then Tim realized that Sebastian was not quite sure of how to use a knife and fork.

"And your father . . . ?" Mrs. Ledger asked.

"Mum!" Pip hissed, interrupting her mother and shaking her head in an attempt to halt this inquisition.

"He's gone away," Sebastian announced tersely.

Mrs. Ledger said, "I am so very sorry, Sebastian. I hadn't meant to pry. It was most rude of me," and she changed the subject.

"That was close," Tim remarked as they went upstairs to his bedroom.

"Your mother is indeed most probing," Sebastian declared, "yet this is the way of mothers. They must be sure of their children's friends."

"Still," Pip said, "I think that'll be the end of the quizzes."

Throughout the night, it rained torrentially, a strong wind blowing down the river valley to drive the rain hard against Pip's bedroom windows, keeping her awake. About midnight, she heard a knock on her bedroom door. It was Tim, who had also been unable to sleep.

"If it keeps on like this," he said, "the river will break its banks by morning. That ditch around the house . . ." he continued.

"You mean the old ha-ha," Pip cut in.

". . . whatever," Tim went on. "It's already filling up like a moat. By morning, it's not going to be a *ha-ha* but an *uh-oh*!"

Pip glanced out of her window. Through the film of rainwater running down the pane, she could see the lights of a downstairs room reflecting on the rising water.

"It's like being in a castle," Tim remarked, "especially with these stone mullions in the windows. All we need now are tapestries hanging from the walls, chain-mail vests in the wardrobe, a court jester with one of those ukulele things . . ."

"A mandolin," Pip corrected him. "Sometimes, Tim, you really are thick."

". . . not to mention a few ditties," Tim continued undeterred, "a couple of manky bear skins spread across the floor and an English longbow or two leaning in a corner with a quiver of arrows."

"How about a damsel in distress?" Pip suggested sarcastically.

"That's you, sis," Tim answered.

"Or an ugly fire-breathing dragon?" Pip went on.

"Still you," Tim added, smiling.

The mention of animal skins spread across the floor brought to Pip's mind a picture of Sebastian's chamber deep underground beneath the house. Suddenly, a spasm of worry ran through her.

"If the water rises much higher," she said anxiously, "what will happen to Sebastian's secret chamber? Or Sebastian? Down there, he won't know the river is rising. He could drown like a rat in a box."

She began gently but insistently tapping on the wall panel. In just a few seconds, the mechanism behind it clicked and it swung open on silent, well-lubricated hinges.

"What concerns you?" Sebastian inquired calmly,

stepping into Pip's room. "Your summons was quite relentless."

"It's been chucking it down for yonks," Tim said.

"Chucking it down? Yonks?" Sebastian repeated. "I am not accustomed to your phraseology."

"It's been raining hard for hours," Tim explained. "The river's going to break its banks and you live underground."

"I appreciate your concern yet I am aware of the water rising," Sebastian said.

"How can you know?" Pip asked. "You hardly have any windows down there."

"Certainly," Sebastian replied, "I have no conventional casements, yet there are other ways to see. Come, follow me."

Sebastian stepped through the opening behind the panel. Pip and Tim followed him, feeling with their feet for the first stones of the flight of steps leading to the passageway, remembering Sebastian's previous warning that the steps were uneven and had been worn away in the middle over the centuries. Once at the bottom of the steps, they carefully followed Sebastian's muffled footsteps along the passage to the heavy oaken door leading into his chamber. As Tim heard the latch open, a faint yellowish light lit up the corridor, illuminating the last five meters or so.

On entering the chamber, it seemed unchanged since their last visit. The glow of the four candles set in their bronze wall mountings glimmered on the vaulting of the ceiling and shone on the series of chains and pulleys suspended from the central stone boss high above. On the oak table, the light touched the pewter bowls and lent a translucence to an alabaster pestle and mortar. The racks of bottles and retorts glittered and the rows of leather-bound books looked as if they had been polished: the gold-leaf embossing of their titles shone as if recently applied.

In the alcove where Sebastian slept, Pip noticed the sheepskin coverings were disturbed and kicked into a pile, suggesting that Sebastian had also been sleeping restlessly. She pressed her hand against the wall to see if it was damp. The stones, although cool, were quite dry. Between the flagstones of the floor there was no sign of any seepage. The air did not smell musty.

"Welcome once again to my humble abode," Sebastian said and, pointing to the wall, continued, "and observe my window on the river."

Protruding from the wall was a horizontally calibrated glass tube containing a red-colored orb.

"This," Sebastian exclaimed, "is connected by a bronze pipe to the river bank. At the far end is a valve. As the river rises, water presses on the valve and the air pressure within the tube increases, forcing the red marker to ascend. The delineation on the glass informs me when the fields are at risk of being inundated. As you can see, this is not presently the case."

"Neat!" Tim exclaimed. "When did you install it?"

"I did not," Sebastian replied. "My father did, as a means of warning when we should bring the animals in from the fields to high ground."

"What about the house?" Pip inquired.

"Be not concerned. The house is never at risk," Sebastian declared confidently. "It was built well above the flood plain. Now," he continued, "I have been studying some of my father's texts. While you are here, let me report something of my findings."

He opened a heavy, leather-bound tome resting on the table. As he did so, Pip and Tim could see its contents consisted of a manuscript written in neat cursive writing upon stiff cream-colored vellum. The ink was faded in places, the capital letters at the start of each paragraph either ornately curled or incorporated into an intricately colored illustration like a medieval religious manuscript. The colors looked as fresh and bright as if they had just been painted. Where gold leaf had been applied to the paint, it shone as if newly refined from its ore.

"My mother illustrated this text for my father," Sebastian remarked.

"What was your mother's name?" Pip asked.

"Lady Tabitha Rawne," Sebastian answered in a soft voice as he ran his finger lightly over an illustration.

Tim tried to make sense of the manuscript.

"You will not understand it, Tim," Sebastian said. "It is written not only in the Latin of my father's day but also in code, indecipherable to all but those with alchemical knowledge."

"What's it about?" Pip inquired.

For a moment, Sebastian was silent. "It is a treatise written by my father," he said at length, "about those who would steal the souls of others. Allow me to demonstrate. Tim, look into my eyes."

Hesitantly, Tim did as he was ordered. In the dim glow of the candle-lit chamber, Sebastian's pupils were dark. Yet, as Tim peered into them, he could see a bright zigzag of luminosity moving within them. It was like looking at the filament of an old-fashioned light bulb swinging from side to side on the end of a flex.

"Now," Sebastian said, "place your hand on the table, fingers spread."

Tim complied. Sebastian removed one of the candles from the candelabrum, tipped it on its side and let the molten wax fall on the table between Tim's fingers. Although Tim's face showed his apprehension, he did not flinch. In fact, he couldn't move his hand at all. It was paralysed.

"Your natural reaction would have been to withdraw your hand so as not to be scalded," Sebastian said. "You were very afraid, yet you did not move your hand for I had control of you. Now, I shall go deeper . . ."

Sebastian stared at Tim. His eyes were wide and intense.

Tim suddenly felt most strange. It was as if his flesh was moving around inside his skin, as if his skin was nothing more than a loose-fitting overcoat several sizes too big. And, within his flesh, there was something else moving sinuously, like a snake searching for a hole in which to hide.

"What's going on?" he asked, but his mouth made no sound. The words echoed within him as if he were shouting in a church.

Sebastian took a small metal clicker from his pocket like the ones found in Christmas crackers. He snapped it once. Tim felt a tiny charge run through his body and his hand lifted from the table as if by its own volition.

"Your soul is now closed to me," Sebastian declared.

"And what did you learn?" Tim asked.

"Much of your basest desires and greatest fears," Sebastian replied. "I will give you an example. You wish your father would give you the money you inherited from your mother's father rather than make you wait until you come of age."

Tim was flabbergasted. He had never mentioned that to anyone, not his father, not Pip — and certainly not Sebastian.

"You see?" Sebastian said. "If I can discover your most precious secrets, I can steal your soul."

As Sebastian was speaking, Pip noticed what she took to be a square glass screen about the area of a hard-backed book mounted on the wall. Displayed in it was a vague moving picture in muted colors.

"What's that?" she said.

"It is a *camera obscura*," Sebastian answered.

"A what?" Tim asked.

"It is an optical device."

"Did your father invent it?"

"Indeed he did not," Sebastian admitted. "The Chinese philosopher M'o Ch'i, five centuries before the time of Our Lord, knew of it. The great Aristotle knew of it also, as did the Arab scholar Alhazen of Basra in the tenth century. However, my father improved upon it and I too have made several minor modifications based upon the writings of Giovanni Battista Della Porta in his publication, *Magiae Naturalis*, published in 1558."

"What does it do, exactly?" asked Pip.

"It captures an image," Sebastian went on, "with the use of a convex lens and projects this onto a flat surface. It is based upon the principle that light travels in a straight line but, when its rays pass through a small hole in a thin material, they do not scatter but cross and re-form as an upside-down image."

"Where's the hole the light comes through from outside?" Tim wanted to know.

"In the attic," Sebastian told him. "The light rays travel down through the house walls in a cavity, guided by prisms."

"What is that a picture of?" Pip asked.

"The fields outside," Sebastian said.

"But how can you see them?" Tim demanded. "First, it's night, and second, it's chucking it down frogs and fishes."

"That was my most difficult modification," Sebastian admitted, "which involved the magnification of all available light to provide enough to form an image. As you can see, I have only partially succeeded, for the image has no color resolution and is not very defined."

"Looks pretty good to me," Tim complimented him. "Certainly as good as those night cameras wildlife documentary makers use."

"What's that?" Pip remarked, peering closely at the screen. "There's something moving in the field."

"Sheep," Tim suggested.

"In this rain?" Pip responded. "They'll be under the hedge, sheltered."

Tim studied the screen and said, "I can't see anything."

"Just there." Pip pointed to the bottom right-hand corner of the screen. "Moving towards the house."

"It is of no consequence," Sebastian announced dismissively.

"But I can see it!" Pip retorted. "And it's not a sheep.

Sheep don't creep along on their bellies." She squinted at the glass plate to get a better view. "It's a dog."

"Look again," Sebastian instructed her, gazing briefly but intently into her face.

Pip peered closer to the screen. The animal moving across the grass was a two-meter-long crocodile, its mouth open, its teeth sharp, its yellowish-green scales polished by the falling rain. As she watched, it reached the ha-ha, and slid down the bank, disappearing under the surface, leaving a flurry in the water.

"Have you ever seen one of these creatures alive in the English countryside?" Sebastian inquired.

"No!" Pip answered emphatically. "Of course not. They live in Africa."

"Precisely," Sebastian answered. "What you saw, Pip, is your chimera, the beast of your fears and nightmares, which I have called up from the depths of your soul."

Once again, he snapped the clicker, handing one to Pip and another to Tim. "You must each have one of these. When you feel your soul being touched by another, press the device just once. It will break the hold upon you. But do not use it frequently. The more you press it, the less power it will retain. Now," he went on, "we have other matters to attend. It is time for us to commence our investigations of Yoland and Master Scrotton. First, we must ascertain the location of their domiciles."

"You mean check out their addresses," Tim replied, putting the clicker safely in his pocket. "Talk modern speak, follow me and prepare to be amazed."

They left Sebastian's subterranean lair and headed for Tim's bedroom. Once there, Tim sat at his computer and accessed the Internet, logging on to the British Telecom site. Twenty seconds after clicking on to Directory Inquiries, Yoland's address appeared on screen: *47, Keats Road*. A search for Scrotton, however, drew a blank.

"He's got to live somewhere," Pip said.

"Is it possible he lives with Yoland?" Tim suggested. "After all, he is his familiar."

"Now that would raise a few eyebrows," Pip remarked.

"Quite," Sebastian concurred. "And neither Yoland nor Scrotton will wish to draw attention to themselves. However, if Scrotton is as I believe him now to be, his place need not be a house."

Pip and Tim stared at each other, flummoxed.

Four

Templum Maleficarum

Sebastian was not walking along the road as they drove to school the following morning. As both Pip and Tim had expected to see him, they cast nervous glances at each other.

"Where's Sebastian today?" Mrs. Ledger remarked.

"Maybe he's farther down the road," Tim suggested. "We did leave a few minutes later than usual."

"He is a most remarkable young man," Mrs. Ledger said. "Well-mannered, obviously clever. Very good-looking, too — the new haircut aside. Where did you first meet him?"

Tim, trying hard to recall if he had been asked this before and, if so, what answer he had offered, said, "When I was fishing."

"Did you?" Mrs. Ledger answered.

Tim, thinking he had given the wrong information, said, "I think so."

"It can't be hard to remember," his mother replied. "You've hardly made many friends since we moved here."

"It's been a long summer," Pip said, defending her brother.

"A lot's gone down," Tim added evasively.

"I should very much like to meet his guardians," Mrs. Ledger continued. "Have you met them?"

"No," Pip admitted, "but we've seen the cousin's husband in the distance with a herd of cows."

As they reached the outskirts of Exington, the traffic became heavier and Mrs. Ledger became a more nervous driver. However, it was not until they were two streets away from the school that she had a fright.

The street was residential, lined by detached houses with trim hedges, neat front lawns and tidy driveways. Dark-green garbage cans stood at the curb, awaiting emptying.

Suddenly, a handsome tabby cat ran out into the street from behind one of the cans. Mrs. Ledger rammed her foot on the brake. The car stopped abruptly, Pip and Tim thrown against their seat belts. From behind came the squeal of tires on tar as another vehicle did an emergency stop to avoid hitting Mrs. Ledger's car. At the sound of the screeching tires, the cat paused, looked at the vehicles, then fled with considerable speed down a driveway. Mrs. Ledger pulled in to the side of the street.

"People really should not have cats if they live in a town," she declared, her hands shaking as she fumbled in her handbag. "They cause accidents and it's unfair to the animals. Cats like fields and woods where they can hunt. Besides, they always get run over." She studied her makeup in the rearview mirror, licking her index finger and tickling the corner of her eye.

"You know, Mum," Pip said, "you're like a cat."

"And how do you make that out, young lady?" her mother retorted.

"Whenever something fazes you, you check your eyeliner or something. Just like a cat. When they're fazed, they wash their faces with their paws."

As they arrived at the school, Sebastian was just entering the main gates, ten paces behind Scrotton.

Catching up with Sebastian, Pip said, "How did you get here ahead of us?"

"But for the stopping capacity of your mother's vehicle . . ." Sebastian began, ignoring Pip's question and leaving the rest of his sentence unspoken.

Pip and Tim exchanged a look.

"You told us you wouldn't shape-shift . . ." Tim said.

"I stated that I could not move around the school in the shape of an animal," Sebastian corrected him. "However, to arrive in the vicinity of the school before the arrival of the pupils and teachers I deem to be of no considerable risk."

"But why did you . . . ?" Pip began.

"I have my reasons," Sebastian cut in on her. "You should not be so inquisitive."

"What were you looking for?" Pip ventured.

"I was looking to see if there was evil hereabouts." Sebastian walked on in silence.

"And?" Tim goaded him.

"Suffice to say I have regrettably discovered nothing of immediate importance." With that, Sebastian walked away, aloof and unapproachable, as if the feline qualities of the cat had yet to wear off him.

During the mid-morning break the library was busy, but Tim was still able to briefly access the librarian's computer, which she had left on. He logged on to the general database and entered Scrotton's name. His age came up as *11*, his address as *14 Peelings Lane, Brampton* and his mother's name as *Mrs. Mary Scrotton*. No father's name was listed.

"He's from a single-parent family," Tim reported as they walked to their next class.

"Or no family at all," Sebastian remarked.

"What do you mean?" Pip asked. "Everyone has parents. They're a biological necessity."

"Not necessarily," Sebastian said enigmatically. "In some cases, such as in that of a . . ."

"A what?" Tim interrupted.

However, at that moment, Scrotton appeared walking towards them and Sebastian ceased talking.

By a row of lockers outside the classroom, Pip noticed a Year Seven girl standing with her left hand thrust deep into her skirt pocket.

As they passed her, a Year Eight girl said spitefully, "You want to watch out for that Julia. She's a witch, she is." She then deliberately fell against the girl, knocking her into the wall. The girl started to sob.

"Is she?" Pip whispered to Sebastian.

He briefly sniffed the air and shook his head.

Pip, Tim, and Sebastian approached the girl. "Why did that dunce-in-a-dress say that?" Pip asked her quietly.

The girl made no reply but half withdrew her hand from her pocket. It was dotted with large warts. "The doctor says I've got too many," she replied in a crestfallen voice. "He can't take them all off at once."

Sebastian leaned casually against the wall next to the girl and, waiting until Scrotton was out of sight, lightly touched her on the neck. She jerked as if she had touched a live wire and stumbled against the lockers. Sebastian moved away and went into the classroom.

"Are you OK?" Tim inquired, pretending to be anxious. The girl was ashen-faced, her hands unsteady: she dropped her books.

"I . . . I think so," she answered. "Something strange just came over me."

"Go to the girls' room," Pip suggested. "Get a drink of water."

Tim, picking up the girl's books, said, "We'll save you a seat."

A few minutes later, as the lesson was beginning, the girl came in and sat beside Pip. She was smiling broadly.

"All right now?" Pip whispered.

"It's really weird," the girl replied. "I can't believe it." She held out her left hand. The skin was completely unblemished, with not so much as a red mark where each wart had been. "They've gone!"

"Strange things, warts," Tim remarked.

Sebastian looked at Pip and winked.

No sooner had Tim arrived home than he hurriedly changed out of his school uniform, pulled his mountain bike out of the garage and pedaled hard in the direction of Brampton. He parked his bicycle against the streetlight outside the hairdresser's, locking the frame to the lamp standard.

Getting directions from the post office, Tim set off down the main street. Between a pub called the White Hart and a baker's shop with an old-fashioned gold-painted Hovis sign hanging over the door, he found a narrow, cobbled lane. Fifty meters along it, just past a small workshop repairing lawnmowers, hedge trimmers and chainsaws, he arrived at the turning into Peelings Lane.

It was an ancient street, little changed in a hundred years. A sluice of running water raced down the center of it which, Tim reckoned, had once served as a communal sewer. The houses on either side were old workers' stone cottages. A few had been renovated, but most were poorly maintained, the paint on the doors flaking, the stonework in need of repair and the gutters cracked. Where summer rainwater had run down the walls hung tendrils of slimy algae. Here and there, clumps of moss grew on the windowsills.

Number fourteen was completely derelict. There was grimy broken glass in most of the windows; the door was rotted through and secured by an ancient, rusty padlock. Tim peered in through the windows. The rooms were completely devoid of furniture, the floorboards warped, damp and mold blotching the walls. A side gate, hanging on one hinge with a cracked plastic number 14 nailed to it, gave on to a minute garden in one corner of which was a long-disused outside lavatory without a roof. Tim squeezed through. The garden was a mass of rank and dying weeds.

Taking care not to snag his jeans on a nail protruding from a window frame lacking a window, Tim clambered into the cottage. Within, it smelled of cat's pee, fungus, and damp plaster. He cautiously climbed the stairs, testing each step before putting his weight on it. The two upper rooms were as empty as those below, save for drifts of dead leaves that had blown in. In one corner, beneath a gaping hole in the ceiling, was a pile of bird and bat droppings.

Tim was about to descend the stairs once more when something on the floor caught his eye. At first, he thought it was a piece of tinfoil that had blown in with the leaves but, as he bent down, he found it was a silver oblong of dirty metal, about two centimeters by one wide. It reminded him of a dog's aluminum collar tag, but thicker and heavier. Rubbing it to clean it, he saw it had been stamped with a symbol: ⊡━

Slipping it into his pocket, Tim left the cottage.

As he came out of the gate on to Peelings Lane, an elderly man appeared, walking falteringly towards him. He wore a tattered flat tweed cap and had a rough-haired mongrel terrier trotting ahead of him on a lead; in his free hand he held a supermarket shopping bag from the top of which hung the green fronds of a bunch of carrots.

"Excuse me," said Tim. "Can you tell me who lives here?"

"Look for yourself, boy!" exclaimed the man sourly. "Nobody lives 'ere. Except them damn cats. It's been empty for at least fifteen years, that 'as."

"Who did live here?" Tim asked politely.

"Ain't no business of yourn," replied the man suspiciously. "What you wan' to know for?"

Tim, thinking fast, said, "I'm . . . I'm doing a project for school. We're looking at who's lived in which houses and how many old families there are in the town."

"Oh! In that case," replied the man, softening his tone, "you've come to the right chap. I can remember all of 'em. This 'ouse . . . Now let me see, nummer . . . nummer . . ." He looked down the lane to count off the houses, ignoring the number on the gate. "Nummer fourteen was lived in by . . ." He paused. "Well, to be quite 'onest, I don't think I can remember who it ever was lived in by. Come to think of it, I don't think it's ever been occ'pied in my lifetime. An' I'm seventy-three an' lived 'ere all me life. It must be, well, I don't know, just one of they things."

"But it must belong to someone," Tim replied, bending down to stroke the mongrel, knowing that this would put him in the old man's favor. "You can't have a whole house with no owner."

The mongrel pushed its head into Tim's hand. Its fur was rough and greasy.

"Like dogs, do you?" the old man inquired.

"Yes," said Tim, to keep the conversation going. "What's his name?"

"'E be Towser," replied the dog's owner, continuing, "can 'appen. You know, when somebody dies an' nobody knows who owns the 'ouse an' they ain't got no relatives, or nobody knows who they are, it just sort of stands there. 'Twas another place like that in Brampton, years since. A small shop, it was. The old lady who owned it emigrated. Australia! That's what they said, anyways. Never seen 'ide nor 'air of 'er since. Suppose that's the case with this 'un. Maybe one day the council'll knock it down."

Tim continued stroking Towser, his fingers getting greasier and greasier. Towser, he considered, certainly needed a bath. Yet Tim knew that as long as he paid attention to the dog he would have its master's attention as well.

"Only thing that lives in there now is them damn cats," the old man continued. "Nasty wretches! Not big, mind you. Lean, sinewy little beggars. Wily as foxes. An' fierce. Fierce as devils, they are! Vicious. Get bit by one of they an' you'll know about it. Now," he went on, warming to the theme, "Towser 'ere is a ratter. Champion ratter. Ain't a rat gets by 'im. 'E's got the courage of ten other terriers. But when it comes to they cats, 'e backs off. I don't blame 'im. They say discretion's the better part of valor. So 'tis for dogs as well as men. I tell you," the old man finished, leaning forward towards Tim as if to prevent one of the cats overhearing him, "if I were a young mum with a little one in a pram, I'd not park it out in my garden anyplace around 'ere. I'm sure they cats'd 'ave the baby."

Out of the corner of his eye, Tim caught a movement on the far wall of the garden. At the same instant, Towser stiffened.

"There's one!" the old man said. "C'mon, Towser! Time we was off."

Without saying goodbye, the old man tugged on Towser's leash and the two of them headed off down the lane at as brisk a pace as the old man could manage.

The cat was a small nondescript animal with no distinguishing marks except a white left forepaw. It made no attempt to move towards Tim but just stood looking at him in the uninterested way cats have. Tim felt strangely uneasy. Glancing up and down Peelings Lane, Tim noticed there was not another creature in sight. He was alone with, he thought to himself, one of the Killer Cats of Brampton.

After a minute, the cat settled down, curling its tail around its hindquarters and closing its eyes.

Tim set off down the lane. At the small workshop, from the murky rear of which he could hear someone unsuccessfully trying to start a lawnmower, he looked back. The cat was following him. Tim had the distinct feeling it was making sure he was leaving the area. Only when he passed the door of the saloon bar of the White Hart did the cat stop and, its tail held jauntily high in the air, make its way back towards Peelings Lane.

"If Scrotton ever plays truant," Tim said later as he, Pip and Sebastian walked across Rawne's Ground towards the Garden of Eden, "the truant officer will be in for a major — like seriously major — shock when he gets to Peelings Lane, and Scrotton'll be boiled in a vat of headmaster's oil."

"He'll never be reported," Pip replied. "Yoland takes attendance, so Yoland decides who's playing hooky. He has only to enter him as present in the book and no one's the wiser."

"As for the house," Tim remarked, "if Scrotton does

live there, I'd not be surprised. It's as filthy as he is. Stink of cats all over the place. Piles of bat poop, dead leaves . . ."

"He does not," Sebastian interjected with certainty. "I believe the house to be a sanctuary."

"A sanctuary?" Pip repeated. "I thought that was a church or something."

"Throughout England," Sebastian went on to explain, "there are places where the wicked may go into hiding for safety. Often, these are caves or hollow trees yet, on occasion, they are buildings. In my father's time, such a place was referred to as a *templum maleficarum* — a sacred precinct of evil."

"Caves I can understand," Tim said. "They last forever. But a house? That can fall down, a builder can repair it . . ."

"Scrotton has given this address because he knows, as a *templum maleficarum*, it will never be repaired," Sebastian said. "If you return in twenty years, it will look exactly the same, protected by the next evil soul to use it. A *templum maleficarum* is often frequented by the powers of evil."

Tim felt his skin crawl. He might, he considered, have bumped into one on the stairs. It was a thought upon which he preferred not to dwell.

"As for the cats," Sebastian added, "they are the guardians of the sanctuary who keep the inquisitive away. You were fortunate not to have had to deal with one of them. They are notoriously vicious."

"I saw one," Tim admitted. "It followed me when I left."

"Did it possess a white left forepaw?"

"Yes," Tim said, the hair on his forearms prickling.

"Then it was a guardian," Sebastian confirmed. "Yet fear not. It will not have pursued you beyond its territory."

They passed the oak bench and, on reaching the river bank, took a narrow path that ran parallel to the river.

"So," Sebastian said, "show me the object you found in the building."

Tim produced the metal oblong, saying, "Probably nothing. Just a gas or electricity meter seal. That sort of thing." He handed it to Sebastian.

On receiving it, Sebastian stopped walking. He studied it very closely then, with a yellowish cloth taken from his pocket, rubbed it vigorously between his finger and thumb. In seconds, the metal gleamed as if it had just been cast.

"Did you notice anything else?" Sebastian inquired.

"Just the bat dung, dead leaves . . ." Tim answered. "Certainly no sign of anyone living there. The house doesn't even have a bathroom. The lavatory's a tumbledown stone shack in the garden." He pointed at the metal oblong. "What is it?"

The sun was lowering towards the horizon, the shadows lengthening. In the fields across the river, a faint mist hovered a few centimeters above the grass.

"The metal from which this is fashioned is an amalgam of platinum, silver and gold," Sebastian announced. "It is known as white gold."

"But what is it?" Pip wanted to know.

"It is a spell key. When some spells are cast, for each part of the spell, there must be a key which acts as a catalyst to start the reaction."

"What is the sign on it?" Pip then asked.

"It is an alchemical symbol referring to a melting furnace."

"But what's a spell key doing in a dump in Brampton?"

"I suspect," Sebastian replied, "that Scrotton has been there and accidentally dropped it."

"If that's so," Tim said, "he'll come back for it and we can follow him . . ."

"He will come at night," Sebastian cut in, "and we can hardly lie in wait for him, hour after hour."

"At least we've got the spell key, not him," Pip said.

"Another will be made with ease," Sebastian stated dismissively and, bringing his arm swiftly back, he tossed the oblong into the middle of the river. It skipped three times like a flat stone, then sank.

"What are you doing!" Tim exclaimed. "It must be worth . . . !"

"It is tainted with evil," Sebastian answered with a shrug, "its value is immaterial and I wish not to possess it."

Five

The Wodwo

Tim pulled up his shorts and made sure the laces of his gym shoes were tight. All about him, thirty Year Seven boys milled around the locker room, changing into their PE clothes, joking and talking loudly. It was their first gym session, and most were eager to begin.

Paying little attention to the hubbub going on around him, Tim concentrated on Scrotton, who had chosen to get changed at the far end of the room, half hidden by an equipment locker. Nevertheless, Tim could still see his clothes were tattered and badly needed laundering.

"Why does Scrotton hide himself?" he whispered to Sebastian, who was wearing Tim's spare clothes.

"When the class ends," Sebastian said, "position yourself so that you might see him. Then, you will come to understand."

One of the gym coaches blew a whistle.

"Form a line!" he commanded in a voice as strident as a sergeant major's.

Cowed into silence, everybody obeyed, following him into the gymnasium. There an obstacle course had been laid out involving wall bars, ropes, a vaulting horse, a parallel beam and some rolling mats in addition to a long row of benches. The gym coach went around the course first to show what was required of the pupils. As he tackled each obstacle, he shouted out his actions in number sequence. Another PE teacher stood by the vaulting horse to help those over it who found the apparatus difficult.

The whistle blew a second time.

"Form a line at the end of the gym!" bellowed the military voice. "At the double!"

The boys instantly complied. Scrotton positioned himself in front of Tim, Sebastian standing behind him.

"You any good at gym?" Scrotton grunted, turning around before they started.

"I don't know," said Tim. "We didn't have a gymnasium at junior school."

"I'm brilliant," said Scrotton arrogantly.

"No doubt," Tim replied sarcastically.

The whistle blew again, and the pupils set off at intervals of about five seconds. When it came to Scrotton's turn, the coach standing at the head of the line said, "Right! Off you go, boy!"

Yet Scrotton did not move. He seemed to be studying the equipment, as if plotting his way around it.

"Get on with it!" the gym coach said impatiently. "It's nothing to be afraid of. I've shown you what to do."

At that point, Scrotton obsequiously said, "Yes, sir, I was just thinking, sir."

With that, he set off at an incredible speed, his agility astonishing. One of the sets of bars was standing at right angles to the wall. The boys had to climb up the bars for six or seven rungs, reach out, get hold of a rope, wrap their legs around it, slide down the rope hand over hand and then run along a bench. Most boys went as fast as they could to the bottom of the bars and then gingerly climbed up the six or seven rungs before tentatively reaching for a rope.

Scrotton, however, did nothing of the sort. He ran straight at the bars, jumped from the ground up to the seventh rung and then, with a leap into mid-air, grabbed hold of a rope and slid down it at an amazing rate. Once he touched the bench below, he set off along it at little less than a sprint. At the end of the bench, he proceeded without pause around the entire course, soon catching up with the boy in front of him and having to wait until he cleared the next obstacle. The teacher by the vaulting horse did not need to help him over it; he rolled perfectly three or four times across the mats, and, when he got to the beam, he simply hoisted himself straight up on it and ran across it as if it were no more than a centimeter above the floor. Eventually, he reached the back of the line again.

Tim, following him around, simply could not keep up, even with his very best efforts. Sebastian took his time.

"That was fast," Tim said with begrudging admiration when he came up to Scrotton at the back of the line.

"Yeah," said Scrotton immodestly. "Told you I was good at gym."

The class continued. In every task that was set for them, one of the games masters stood by the apparatus to assist the inexperienced or prevent injury: Scrotton required no help or guidance. He was nimble, swift and incredibly agile. Several times, Tim caught sight of the teachers looking at each other with surprise.

The gym period over, Tim made sure he was first into the locker room where he positioned himself so that he could see behind the lockers. Sebastian held back. Scrotton came in and, believing he was not being observed, swiftly removed his undershirt and tugged on it as quickly as he could. Yet Tim still saw a thin ridge of tightly matted black hair down Scrotton's spine. Across his shoulders, he was also very hairy. His arms were dark with hair but it was much shorter and seemed to have been cut.

"Ape-lout!" muttered a voice over Tim's shoulder.

He turned to find the boy who had told him about Scrotton on the first day of term.

"You should have seen him in junior school," the boy went on. "If there was a tree, he was up it, swinging by his arms like a scruffy little Tarzan. The teachers were forever chasing him off the infants' climbing bars."

"You don't know where he lives, do you?" Tim asked.

"No. Never saw his parents, not on open evenings or anything. We used to say he wasn't born but made out of a packet of Insta-Fool." The boy grinned. "Just add water and stir."

For the remainder of the morning, Tim and Sebastian tended not to watch Scrotton to avoid arousing his suspicion. Instead, Pip turned her attention his way.

In class Scrotton was clumsy. He was continually restless, tapped his fingers on the desktop and jiggled his foot. His attention span seemed to last little more than a minute. When he wrote in his exercise book, he held his cheap plastic ballpoint pen between his second and third fingers instead of his index finger and thumb, writing with his hand curved and arched around with the pen pointing in towards him. His writing was scrawling and he stuck his tongue out when faced with a difficult question, licking his lips and frowning, reminding Pip of an iguana. She also noticed he frequently put one of his hands inside his shirt to scratch his stomach.

Close up, his skin was sallow and there were spots with large blackheads in them on the back of his neck. His filthy fingernails were long, as thick as horn and split in places, more like claws than ordinary fingernails. The lines of his palms were ingrained with dirt. The skin behind his ears was flaky and gray. His clothes were disheveled, his unpolished leather shoes scuffed, a line of dried mud along the edge of the soles.

Pip also noticed he had very few of the kinds of possessions the other pupils owned. He did not have a mobile phone nor even wear a wristwatch. His pencil case was just an old wooden cigar box held shut with a perished rubber band, the words *Cuba Corona* printed on the lid. His calculator was an old solar-powered Casio, the casing held together with peeling tape.

All the while Pip was, as Tim put it, *on Scrotton's case*, Sebastian decided to discover what he could about Yoland. As the head of chemistry was teaching a double-period senior-school class in the chemistry laboratory until lunch break, Sebastian reasoned he was very unlikely to come out of his laboratory and so, waiting until the school had settled down to the timetable, he excused himself from the class they were in and headed for the staffroom.

Knocking lightly on the door, Sebastian entered without waiting for a response. Inside, three or four teachers were sitting around a large table, marking exercise books. Another lounged in a battered chair, reading a newspaper, a mug of tea balanced on the arm.

Against a long wall stood a rank of large wooden pigeonholes, each bearing a name card in a tarnished brass holder. Sebastian walked calmly across to them, soon finding Yoland's. He was about to start looking in it when the teacher reading the paper put it down and said, "What do you think you're doing, boy?"

Sebastian had to think fast and, casting a quick glance at the pigeonhole next to Yoland's, read the label on it.

"Miss Williams asked me to get a book for her," he said.

"Next one over," the teacher replied, "and don't just barge in. Wait at the door." He resumed reading his newspaper.

"Thank you, sir," Sebastian replied, yet he continued to look in Yoland's pigeonhole.

There was nothing of interest in it: some Year Eight answer sheets, a few textbooks, a box of pencils and markers and some teaching notes and printed examination papers.

At lunch break, Pip bought Sebastian a pack of tuna and cucumber sandwiches and a carton of orange juice. Sebastian bit into the sandwich, chewed briefly upon it and swallowed: then he reached over and read the label on the packet.

"What is tuna?" he asked.

"A large fish," Pip told him.

"And cucumber?"

"A sort of vegetable," Tim replied after a moment's thought, "but keep your voice down. You'll be branded a weirdo if you don't know what a cucumber is."

"Do you like it?" Pip inquired.

Sebastian considered for a moment and began, "It has a most piquant . . ."

"It's wicked," Tim interrupted.

Sebastian smiled and replied, "It's cool."

At that moment, Yoland appeared in the dining hall carrying the Year Eight answer sheets Sebastian had seen in the pigeonhole. At his arrival, the hubbub died down a little only to become louder a few moments later. Yoland chose a table at the far end of the room, bought himself a coffee, sat down and started to mark the answer sheets.

"He's on lunch duty," Pip said.

"What a chance!" Tim exclaimed. "We've got him for the next forty minutes."

Tall, thin and with a lean face, Yoland moved with an almost insect-like precision, reminding Pip of a pale green, giant praying mantis she had seen on a wildlife documentary. His hands had very long, bony fingers ending in nails that were trim and neat. They looked as if they had been buffed by a manicurist. His graying hair was thick around the sides of his head, his nose and chin sharp, his eyes always on the lookout for trouble. He wore a trimly tailored pinstriped suit, which was quite unusual because most of the teachers chose more casual clothes, and he also wore a tie with a college crest on it. His legs were long and thin, his ears flat against the side of his head, with, on this occasion, his hair curled neatly behind them. He looked, Tim considered, fastidious, a typical scientist, a man fascinated by intricate details.

When he walked around the dining hall, he did so in an almost upright fashion, not leaning forward but striding out as if his legs were determined to go first, his body following without any choice. Whenever he turned his head it was with a quick motion, like that of a wary lizard.

And, whenever he approached their table on his occasional patrol of the room, the pendant vibrated.

After they had finished their lunch, Sebastian suggested they go out into the playground, where he led them to the farthest point from the school buildings. There, a centuries-old horse chestnut tree stood on the boundary of the playing fields, the grass beneath it scattered with conkers.

"If Yoland needs a familiar, he must be up to something serious," Tim reasoned.

"It is on the subject of Scrotton," Sebastian said, "that I wished us to come outside." He looked around to ensure Scrotton was out of earshot.

Tim, recalling the boy's Tarzan comment and Scrotton's performance in the gym, looked into the branches of the horse chestnut above them. Scrotton was nowhere to be seen.

"Now that I have seen Scrotton's nimble demonstration in the gymnasium," Sebastian began, "I am convinced, as my father once suspected, that Scrotton is a wodwo."

"A wod what?" Tim exclaimed.

"A wodwo," Sebastian repeated. "It is a word long lost from the English language and very difficult to explain. It is — or was — a creature that lives in the forest."

"The Monkey Man of the Woods!" Tim joked, swinging an arm over the back of his head, gripping his chin and grunting.

"Tim's jest may be nearer the truth than you expect," said Sebastian. "A wodwo is not entirely human, nor yet animal. It has the cunning and instincts of a wild beast, but," he went on, "where Scrotton is concerned, because of his time spent in the company of humans, he has acquired many human attributes and much intelligence. Furthermore, as a familiar, he has also gained much alchemical or magical knowledge. This wodwo, therefore, unlike most, is a very dangerous creature."

At that moment, they caught a glimpse of Scrotton across the playground. He had a small, thin boy in a neck lock and was repeatedly punching his upper arm.

"As you may see for yourself," Sebastian declared, "the bestial in him comes forth when the human retreats."

Six

A Burrow and a Book

The next afternoon, Pip, Tim and Sebastian watched through the library window as Scrotton set off through the school gates, carrying his scruffy bag. As soon as he was out of sight, they left the school and followed at a discreet distance.

Walking briskly, he headed out of the town and along the road towards Brampton. At a point where the road and the river went past a steep wooded hill, Scrotton suddenly veered right through the trees along a barely discernible trail that might have been made by deer or foxes. His pace did not slow even as the hillside grew progressively steeper. Pip, Tim and Sebastian, hiding their school bags under a thicket of brambles, followed him through the trees, taking care not to step on fallen twigs. Yet it seemed that Scrotton was oblivious to them and kept on ascending the hill, keeping to the path. Squirrels, busy here and there burying nuts, paid him no heed. Pheasants, pecking around in the leaf litter, merely looked up then continued their foraging.

"Notice," Sebastian said quietly, "how the animals are not afeared of him, for he is one of them."

Three hundred meters up the hill stood a vast oak tree. Tim reckoned it had to be at least a thousand years old. Leaving the path, Scrotton headed straight for it, scuffing his feet behind every step to erase his tracks.

Nearby was the substantial trunk of a fallen beech tree. Sebastian quickly crouched behind it, signaling to Pip and Tim to do likewise. Beneath the oak was what looked like a badger's sett, fresh earth turned out from between the roots. As they watched, Scrotton got down and thrust his schoolbag into the hole. Then, with the agility of a snake, he slithered in after it. They saw his shoes disappear into the darkness of the cavity.

"What on earth is that?" whispered Pip.

"I don't know about what *on* earth it is," Tim said quietly. "It seems he's gone *to* earth."

"This is his place," Sebastian said softly.

Tim asked, "Why doesn't he live in that old house?"

"He is ill at ease in houses," explained Sebastian. "Here he feels safe."

"What now?" Pip pondered.

"We bide our time," said Sebastian. "He will be out shortly for it will be night in an hour or two and he must find food."

Sure enough, ten minutes later, Scrotton reappeared. The first they saw of him was his face peering through the entrance to the tunnel, looking around like a wary animal assessing whether or not it was safe to exit. Finally, he wriggled out of the sett, no longer wearing his school uniform but a pair of muddy jeans and a soiled brown sweatshirt. Turning, he went up the hill, over the brow and disappeared into the depths of the wood.

"Now is our chance," said Sebastian. "Pip, keep

guard. Call to us if he returns. But softly. Do not alarm him. Tim, come with me."

At the entrance, Sebastian handed Tim what looked like a ball of dark-blue gum the size of a cherry.

"As long as we are within, chew upon this." He placed another piece in his own mouth, his cheek bulging. "Now, let us descend into the lair of the wodwo."

Two meters in, it was pitch dark, only a glimmer of late afternoon light seeping in through the entrance. Tim blinked to try to adjust his eyes but with no success. However, as soon as he put the ball of gum in his mouth, it was as if he was wearing a pair of military night goggles. The interior of the sett was immediately bathed in a pale glow.

"Hey! Cool!" he exclaimed. "What's in this stuff?"

"Extract of carrot," Sebastian replied, "and a few other ingredients of which you are to remain ignorant."

The tunnel was about a meter wide and high, with a right-angle bend approximately four meters in. The walls were of earth with, here and there, the massive roots of the oak above supporting them. In places, they were polished where Scrotton had rubbed against them in passing. Beyond the bend, it carried on for at least another eight meters. The earth of the floor was smooth and as hard as concrete, while the roof was loose and held together by a dense network of small roots, some of which hung down like inanimate tendrils.

At the far end of the tunnel was a larger chamber, the roof reinforced with intertwined sticks, the walls containing small cut-away shelves upon which Scrotton had placed his school books. Into one, he had jammed his school uniform. Towards the back was a large pile of brown leaves and bracken to serve as a bed. Beside it was a dented aluminium bowl of brackish water.

"He really does live like an animal," Tim commented. "How long do you think he's been here?"

"Several centuries," Sebastian answered.

"Several centuries!" Tim replied with amazement. "And no one's found him?"

"Why should they?" Sebastian said. "They believe this to be a badger sett."

"But what about hunters? People with dogs? They used to kill badgers. Or government agricultural officials? They gas badgers because they think they carry tuberculosis to cattle."

"Yes," Sebastian concurred, "but Scrotton is not a badger. He will have killed any dogs that entered his den, and on occasion the men who accompanied them, too. There will be many skeletons in the woodland . . ."

Tim's stomach muscles tightened with fear. Suddenly, what had seemed little more than a prank was now a deadly dangerous situation. He thought immediately of Pip outside.

"Will we be long?" he asked Sebastian nervously.

"We shall be but minutes," Sebastian announced. He rummaged in the bed of bracken, pulling out from under it a wooden box, the corners strengthened with dull brass brackets, the hasp sealed with an ancient but well-lubricated padlock.

"Right! Let's go!" Tim said. "We can open it back home."

"That is not possible," Sebastian stated, placing the box on the earthen floor. "If we steal the box, Scrotton will find it in our possession. It will call him to its side. Even now, I am sure it is telling him someone is tampering with it in his absence."

"So what do we do?" Tim asked agitatedly.

"Open it," Sebastian replied, "as rapidly as we may."

"We don't have the key," Tim responded, looking fervently around the chamber.

Sebastian closed his eyes, cupping his hands around the padlock. There was a metallic click and the hasp of the padlock parted.

"Nice one!" Tim exclaimed.

"It is but a single-lever mechanism," Sebastian replied, "and requires little skill."

Opening the box, Sebastian removed a small, leather-bound book, the cover blotched with mold, the spine cracked with age.

"What is it?" Tim asked, his fear momentarily forgotten.

Sebastian opened the book at random, swiftly turning over page after page before announcing, "It is a compendium of spells known as *The Book of Gerbert d'Aurillac.*"

"Who?"

"I will tell you of him anon," Sebastian replied.

Tim moved nearer to peer into the box. Reaching out, he asked eagerly, "What else is there?"

"Touch nothing!" Sebastian said sharply, pushing Tim's hand aside. "Scrotton must not know we have been here." He carefully replaced the book.

When he saw them, Tim was aghast at the other contents: a lamb's skull, some cow's teeth, the russet tail of a fox, a snake's skin and what he assumed from their color were two dried crows' wings. It was not until Sebastian began to close the box that Tim noticed an object about the size of a small child's clenched fist, black and studded all over with small protruding nails like panel pins.

"What's that?" Tim exclaimed.

"That," Sebastian replied, "is a heart."

Tim was momentarily silent. The vision of a gamekeeper or a man naively walking his dogs through the woods on a fine summer's afternoon entered his mind. This was quickly followed by an image of Pip crouching behind the fallen log, Scrotton creeping up on her unawares.

"A human heart?" he asked querulously.

"No," Sebastian answered. "It is a canine heart."

"Why is it studded with nails?"

"This is a method," Sebastian stated, "of protection against any others of its kind."

He closed the box and put it back under the bracken. They headed on all fours for the sett entrance.

On reaching the right-angle bend, Sebastian ordered Tim to wait while he went ahead to signal to Pip and ensure Scrotton was nowhere in sight.

Tim, with some reluctance, agreed. He sat on the hard earth floor with his back to the wall, his arms clasping his knees.

After a few moments, he had the uncanny feeling between his shoulder blades that he was being watched. He glanced down the tunnel towards the chamber. There was nothing there. Looking the other way, he could make out Sebastian's shape in the tunnel entrance, silhouetted against the light.

It was then something wet touched his neck. He reached up, thinking it was a drip of water from the soil above. His fingers met something thin, soft and damp: yet the moment he touched it, it was gone. Looking over his shoulder, there was nothing to be seen except a tiny hole in the tunnel wall.

"All clear?" he asked Sebastian in a stage whisper.

Sebastian gestured for him to stay put.

Just as Tim signaled his understanding, something slimy fell on his head, rolled off and briefly wrapped it-self around his ear before dropping to the floor.

Instantaneously, the roof of the tunnel became fes-tooned with gigantic earthworms, dangling from holes like obscene Christmas decorations. Shiny with slime, pink and brown, they writhed to and fro as if searching for him, tasting the air for him, pointing at him as if to tell the others where he was, a clump of them over his head fingering down towards his scalp. Two detached themselves from the roof and started to intertwine with his hair. He clawed at them, pulling them free only to find others had replaced the first. His hands were slick with their translucent mucus.

Disregarding Sebastian's order, Tim scrambled towards him. Just as he arrived at his side, Pip frantically beck-oned to them. Running at a crouch, they made for the fallen beech, leaped over it and lay flat. In less than a minute, Scrotton came jogging down the hill, occa-sionally dropping to all fours and moving forward like a chimpanzee. He paused at the tunnel entrance, looked furtively around, then vanished into it. They waited five minutes then, as cautiously but as rapidly as possible, made for the road, collected their school bags from under the brambles and speedily headed home.

"So who's this d'Aurillac?" Tim inquired as he and Pip settled down that evening on two stools, facing Sebastian across the table in his underground chamber.

Sebastian stretched, crossed his arms and, leaning on the table, began, "Gerbert d'Aurillac was born in the mountains of the Auvergne in France, in the tenth century. His date of birth and his original family name are not exactly known, nor is his background, but he is believed to have come from lowly stock.

"In the middle of that century, he became a Benedictine monk at the monastery of St. Gerald at Aurillac, hence the name by which he became known. About a decade later, he was sent by his abbot to Spain to study the *quadrivium*, the four subjects of arithmetic, music, astronomy, and geometry. After attending to his studies in the libraries of the cathedral of Vic and the monastery of Ripoll, he visited Cordoba, the capital of southern Spain, which was then ruled by Muslim Arabs. Very cultured and learned in mathematics, astronomy, and astrology, they possessed a library of many thousands of books."

"I don't understand something," Pip interrupted. "If he was a Christian monk, how could he go to an Islamic land?"

"In that time," Sebastian explained, "Christian and Muslim men were not enemies as later they were to become in the Crusades."

"So where does his book fit in?" asked Tim.

Sebastian went on, "In Cordoba, Gerbert studied under a famous Muslim magician whose considerable magical power was based upon spells recorded in a volume locked in an iron strongbox. Realizing this, Gerbert seduced the magician's daughter, promising to take her away and marry her if she helped him acquire the book. She drugged her father, removed the key from his person and, unlocking the chest, gave the book of spells to Gerbert."

"And they lived happily every after?" Pip suggested.

"Indeed not," Sebastian continued. "Gerbert fled, leaving the girl behind. When her father regained his consciousness, he was enraged and set off in pursuit, but Gerbert succeeded in escaping him."

"Sounds like a real jerk," said Tim vehemently.

"There is, I fear, more," Sebastian added. "It is said Gerbert prayed to Satan to save him from the magician, and that he bartered his soul to the Devil and that Satan promised him even greater powers than were in the book of spells. For the remainder of his life, Gerbert was said to keep a human head, presented to him by Satan, with which he conversed, learning many more evil secrets which he added to the book."

"And Scrotton's got the book," Tim said.

"In the year of Our Lord 983," Sebastian said finally, "Pope Otto the Second appointed Gerbert as abbot of a famous monastery and in the year 999, he was elected Pope Sylvester the Second."

"Cosmic!" Tim remarked. "A pope who sold himself to Satan and owned a book of the Devil's personal spells."

"More to the point," Pip half whispered, "if Scrotton's got it now, Yoland's got it, too."

For some minutes, Sebastian was silent. Finally, he stood up and declared, "I feel assured now that Yoland is not concerned with the creation of a homunculus, the transmutation of iron into gold or the perfection of *aurum potabile*. For these, he would have no use of the book."

"Then what?" ventured Tim.

"I know not yet," Sebastian admitted, "but you may be assured it is more evil and ambitious than anything of which Malodor could have dreamed."

Tim's first attempt at a sick note was superb. Modelling his writing on his mother's, it read, *Please excuse Sebastian from school today. He has a badly upset stomach. Yours, Anna Gillette.* Then, after practicing the signature, he incorrectly signed it *Annette* and had to start again. Eventually, with it finished, he folded it into an envelope and wrote, *B. Yoland Esq.* on the front.

"If Yoland asks, I'll tell him your mother asked me to deliver it."

"Are you sure this will be sufficient?" Sebastian asked as they waited in Tim's room for Pip to finish putting on her uniform.

"Course," Tim replied. "They don't check if it's true. At least, not unless you keep on falling ill. Then they give your parents a ring. But for a one-off? No problemo! Now," he went on, "don't forget. Our dad's out on business and Mum's going to get her hair done after she drops us off. If the telephone rings in the house three times, then stops, then rings once, it means Scrotton's in school."

"And if it rings twice, pauses, then rings twice again, he is *in absentia*," Sebastian said.

"You've got it!" Tim retorted, checking that his mobile phone was fully charged.

Half an hour later, Pip and Tim walked through the school gates ten paces behind Scrotton, who looked as scruffy as ever and carried his tattered sports bag with the handles slung over his shoulder. At the bicycle racks, Tim paused and made the pre-arranged call. Once in the classroom, he put the sick note upon the register where it lay on the demonstration bench.

Back at Rawne Barton, Sebastian shape-shifted into a crow and flew off in the direction of the woods, arriving at the oak tree within ten minutes. Once perched on a stout bough, he cawed three times. It was not inconceivable that Scrotton had stationed a sentry, especially if he had sensed his burrow had been recently visited. Yet nothing seemed out of the ordinary, so Sebastian glided to the woodland floor and started to strut about in the jaunty way of crows. A squirrel seemed momentarily interested in his presence but, listening to its intermittent squeaking and churring noises, and watching as it collected twigs, dead leaves and lengths of shredded bark, Sebastian realized it was intent on constructing a nest in a nearby ash tree and protecting it from another squirrel which was busy burying nuts.

Satisfied that Scrotton had stationed no guards, Sebastian stepped behind the oak, transformed himself back into human form and approached the burrow entrance. Placing a piece of the blue gum in his mouth, he lowered himself into the cavity. To avoid the worms, he pulled himself quickly forward on his elbows until he reached Scrotton's chamber, where he felt under the bed of bracken, lifted out the box, sprang the padlock and opened it. Very carefully, he removed the book of spells and began to read, his eyes moving quickly over the archaic text. Every now and then, he looked up and scanned the burrow to ensure he was still alone.

The spells, mostly written in Latin or Middle French, dealt with a wide variety of subjects, from simple curses against individuals to complex ceremonials that could purportedly destroy a nation or bring down a kingdom. However, one in particular drew Sebastian's attention. It involved a complicated four-part process but this, however, was not what initially caught his eye. The page was bookmarked with a dead oak leaf.

Sebastian memorized the spell then, returning the book to the box, locked it, slid it back into its hiding place and set about a thorough fingertip search of the burrow.

Meanwhile, at Bourne End Comprehensive, Tim and Pip — and Scrotton — were in a double period of geography, commencing a project on Africa. The first forty-five minutes of the class involved watching a video. Halfway through, Pip nudged Tim. Scrotton was clearly very agitated. He wriggled in his seat, fumbled with his books and ballpoint pen and tapped his feet on the rung of his chair.

He knows, Pip wrote for Tim in her notebook.

Tim nodded.

At the end of the lesson, the bell for the mid-morning break rang. In a second, Scrotton was out of his seat as if it were red hot and heading for the door.

"Excuse me!" the geography teacher called after him. "We wait until . . ."

Scrotton was already out of the door and heading down the corridor.

"He's going to the woods!" Tim muttered. "We've got to stop him. Get my books."

Tim followed hard on Scrotton's heels but, as Scrotton made for the science department and his locker, Tim headed for the playground and the main school entrance. It was, he knew, the only way into or out of the school grounds during lessons: all the other gates were kept locked.

A minute later, Scrotton appeared halfway across the playground, carrying his bag. Tim ran hard at him, deliberately slamming into him, knocking him off his feet to sprawl across the concrete.

"I don't like you," he said loudly as Scrotton got to his feet. "You're ugly, you smell like a dung heap, you're a bully and," he added in case these insults were insufficient to raise Scrotton's anger, "you're a big-headed, poisonous little dwarf."

Scrotton dropped his bag and launched himself into midair, clenching his fists. He swung a punch at Tim's head. Tim weaved aside but still took a painful hit on his shoulder. Scrotton spun around and came at him again, hurling himself on to Tim's back with the ferocity of a leopard leaping onto an antelope. Tim felt Scrotton's hot stinking breath on his neck. His short legs quickly wrapped about his waist, and his arms locked around his chest. For a moment, Tim thought that, had Scrotton not been wearing shoes, his toes would have linked together like a monkey's, to tighten their grip.

"Think you're clever, don't you?" Scrotton muttered into Tim's ear, flecks of spit spraying on to Tim's cheek and into his ear. "You don't know nothing, you don't! Nothing!" Scrotton spat, a gob of warm, glutinous saliva slithering down Tim's neck and under his collar. "You're'n ignoramus!"

"And you're a moron," Tim rejoined as he reached over his head, grabbed Scrotton's collar and, leaning forward, tried to tug him over his head as a television wrestler might, to slam him on the ground. Yet Scrotton's legs prevented the ploy and Tim realized that he was in a losing position. His only hope was to fall and try and get on top of Scrotton, but when he attempted this maneuver, Scrotton leaned the other way to maintain their balance.

By now, a jostling crowd of both boys and girls had gathered around the fight. Most were egging Tim on. Some shouted insults at Scrotton from the safety of the mass. Pip came up, trying to push her way through to help Tim, but the throng was too tightly packed.

Suddenly, Tim felt Scrotton's teeth nibbling on the side of his neck and he knew, if Scrotton succeeded, he would bite through his jugular and he would bleed to death before any ambulance could arrive.

"Right!" shouted a voice. "You two stop this this very instant!"

Scrotton still clung onto Tim's back, but his teeth halted their searching.

Standing in front of them was one of the teachers on playground duty, a cup of coffee in his hand. He had clearly spilled much of it in his hurry to arrive on the scene.

"Break it up! Now! Separate yourselves!" He nudged Scrotton's bag with his foot. "Whose is this?"

"Mine," said Scrotton.

"Mine, sir!" snapped the teacher. "Pick it up. You two follow me."

A few minutes later, Tim and Scrotton stood side by side in front of the headmaster's desk. The teacher on duty recounted what had happened. Dr. Singall leaned back in his chair and surveyed them both.

"This kind of behavior is not tolerated at Bourne End Comprehensive," he announced sternly. "I will not condone fighting. Scrotton, you will spend the remainder of the day sitting on a chair outside my office where I can keep an eye on you and where you will do work set by your teachers. At lunch break, you will accompany Mr. Taylor here wherever he goes on duty. That will keep the two of you apart and give you a chance to cool down." He looked at Tim. "And you, Ledger, will attend your classes and, tomorrow morning, will present me with a 300-word essay on why you think I will not condone fighting."

The bell rang for the start of classes.

"And bear in mind," Dr. Singall said finally, "if there is a repetition of this, I shall call your parents in. Now, both of you get out."

"Well?" Pip asked as she met Tim in the corridor outside their next lesson.

"Scrotton's doomed," he replied. "Tied by a leash to the teacher or a chair outside the headmaster's office."

"And you?"

"Only got an essay to write. The head clearly doesn't like Burrow Boy."

That evening, after completing their homework and Tim's punishment essay, Tim and Pip tapped on the panel and, accompanied by Sebastian, descended to his chamber.

When Tim told Sebastian what had occurred at school, Sebastian smiled and said, "You did well, Tim, and at considerable risk to yourself. Scrotton is not to be meddled with, for he would assuredly have bitten deep into your neck had he had the opportunity."

"If he had," Tim replied, "I would've bled to death."

"Yes," Sebastian concurred. "Thus have you earned my eternal gratitude. Had he apprehended me in the woods, I could have shared a similar fate."

"But surely he wouldn't . . ." Pip began.

"Be assured he would," Sebastian interrupted. "Remember, he is a wodwo and, as such, is not guided by common morality. To him there is no distinction between right or wrong, good or evil. As with any animal, there is only survival."

"What about your visit to Scrotton's hole?" Tim inquired.

Sebastian unfolded a square of heavy paper.

"This is the spell upon which I am certain Yoland is concentrating his efforts," he declared. "I memorized it from the book. Translated into modern English, it is entitled: To Captivate the Minds of Many."

"You mean," Tim said, "it's a spell Yoland can use to control minds?"

"Indeed," Sebastian concurred. "At present, he may have the power to see into a person's soul but he has yet to fully develop the ability to take complete control over it. This spell will give him that." Sebastian folded the sheet of paper and slipped it into one of his father's volumes for safekeeping.

"How can you be certain this is the one?" Pip asked.

"First," Sebastian replied, "Scrotton had marked the page. Second, it is a four-part spell requiring four keys, one of which you found in the dilapidated house, Tim. Third, in closely searching the burrow, I have discovered the other three thrust into the soil of the roof."

From his pocket, Sebastian produced several other squares of paper, spreading them on the table. Upon each of them he had drawn an esoteric symbol.

"These are engraved on the keys," he began.

The first was the symbol: ◎

"This," Sebastian explained, "refers to divinity and power. It is the symbol from which Christians derived the halo. However, the divinity need not be that of Our Lord but also of the powers of darkness."

The second bore the emblem: ⊕

"It was first used," Sebastian stated, "by the ancient Greeks to represent the world. It is today still used by astrologers to represent the world upon which we live."

On the last was: ‑⦵‑

"This," he paused to allow its significance to sink in, "is the symbol for the essence of the human soul."

"What were the keys made of?" Tim inquired.

"The first of gold, the second of silver, the last of platinum."

"And the furnace key which Tim found is made of all three," Pip remarked. "That must be the most important."

"A furnace, power, the world and the soul," Tim thought aloud. "Mix them all together in a cauldron with eye of bat and toe of toad and what do you have . . . ?"

"Without your fanciful additions," Sebastian replied, "a grand and terrifying ambition."

Seven

A Bungalow Like Any Other — Not!

"Yoland's house," Tim considered as they sat at a table in the dining hall, "is going to be easier said than done." He bit into an apple. "Scrotton's hole only had guardian worms." He winced at the thought. "It didn't have doors and windows with locks. And while it's true that as long as we're in school, so is Yoland, and therefore we know where he is, I don't see how we can take advantage of that. We certainly can't risk the sick-note scam again so soon and we can hardly stake the joint out. What's more, Scrotton must have told his master that someone had searched his burrow on the day Sebastian supposedly had the runs. If we're not careful, Yoland'll put two and two together and make 193."

"Two plus two equals four," Sebastian interrupted, perplexed by Tim's arithmetic. "And what are the runs?"

"Use your imagination," Tim retorted.

"Surely if we do get in," Pip added, "won't he have a warning system like Scrotton has?"

"Assuredly," Sebastian answered, which did little to allay Pip's uneasiness.

They were still contemplating the problem an hour later when, during a library study session, the answer to it fell into their laps.

Halfway through the period, a Year Nine boy entered, handing a slip of paper to the librarian, who briefly perused it then announced, "Notice from the headmaster. Due to an emergency staff meeting, classes will end ten minutes early today. Pupils are to vacate the grounds as quickly as possible and by four o'clock at the latest. School buses will arrive ten minutes early. Only those involved in the soccer trials may remain on school property, congregating in the gym. It is hoped the trials will commence at five-fifteen."

"You know what this means?" Pip whispered from behind a book on the history of costume. "For as long as the staff meeting lasts, Yoland will be here. And we've got until about a quarter past five."

"How so?" Tim replied.

"Think, dumbo!" Pip came back at him. "The team trials don't start until five-fifteen when the staff leave the meeting."

No sooner was the lesson over than Tim phoned his mother on his mobile phone and asked her if he, Pip and Sebastian could go to the cinema straight after school. She agreed and said she would pick them up at eight o'clock at Burger King, giving Sebastian a lift as well. "Sure thing!" he answered and hung up.

Mounted on the corridor wall by the school secretary's office was a map of the town and the surrounding countryside, color-coded to show the streets and areas from which the school drew its pupil intake. Tim quickly identified Keats Road, a suburban street across the other side of the town and just outside the school's district.

"It won't be wise for us to approach or leave the place together," Tim decided. "A threesome might attract attention."

"And," Pip added, "if we meet Yoland when we're on our way back, one can offer an excuse easier than three."

They each studied a different route, memorizing it.

When the final bell rang, Sebastian hung back to watch as Yoland headed for the lecture theatre where the staff meeting was being held. Pip made sure Scrotton was on his way to his burrow while Tim joined the trail of pupils walking home through the town, the number growing thinner the farther it went from the school.

One street away from Keats Road, Tim went into a corner shop, bought himself a large Mars bar and lingered around outside eating it until the others caught up with him.

Pip looked at her watch. "Four-twenty," she stated. "To be on the safe side, we've got forty minutes."

They made off down Keats Road. It was a quiet suburban street lined with laburnum and lime trees. Every so often along the roadside, there was a sandpit for dogs. The buildings mostly dated from the 1930s or 1940s, semi-detached houses with pebble-dashed walls; a few were bungalows of the same age. The gardens were neat, the flowerbeds well-kept, hedges trimmed, lawns mown and gates painted. Most of the properties had garages at the end of short concrete drives.

Number forty-seven was a bungalow that looked no different from any of the others. It had a dark slate roof, the walls rendered and painted white. The front door and windows were obviously new, made of white PVC and double-glazed.

Checking up and down the street that no one was observing them, they slipped one by one through the garden gate, pushed their school bags under a holly bush and set off to walk around the bungalow on a small gravel path which encircled it. Their every step crunched on the stones underfoot.

"Nifty early-warning system," Tim remarked.

The rear garden was lined with a tall privet hedge that prevented any neighbors from seeing what they were doing.

The curtains on all the windows but one were open. Through them, they could see the lounge contained a settee, a low table with a glass top, an armchair and a television. Against one wall stood a bookshelf lined with chemistry textbooks. In the dining room was a modern dining table and four chairs while in the bedroom there was a double bed and a chest of drawers, a wardrobe and two chairs. The kitchen was basic — a gas range, a fridge and a washing machine installed under the work surface. Against one wall stood a kitchen table and two chairs.

"You know," Pip remarked, "it doesn't look — I don't know — lived in. There's no pictures or ornaments."

"He is a fastidious man," Sebastian said as if in explanation.

"Never mind Yoland's neatness," Tim said. "How do we get in?" He pointed to the window latches. "Even they've got key-operated locks." He glanced at Sebastian. "How about you do your padlock trick?"

"I fear I cannot," Sebastian answered. "To do so, I must hold the lock in my hand."

"So that's it," Pip decided. "We can't get in without smashing a window or something."

As she was speaking, Tim set off to walk around the bungalow a second time. Where an old garage abutted the house, there grew a tall, dense buddleia bush, the conical flower heads gone to seed. Parting the tangle of branches and peering through them, he could make out a small wood-framed window, the sill rotted through, the paint peeling and the glass hazy with dirt. Pressing his face to the pane, he surveyed the interior of the garage and returned to the others.

"We're in!" he announced, grinning broadly. "There's a window in the garage and a door from the garage into the house."

"It's going to be a tight fit," Pip remarked when she saw the window. "You shouldn't've pigged out on that Mars bar."

Tim tested the window. The latch was shut.

"Return to square one," Pip said.

"Watch and wait, listen and learn," said Tim pontifically.

The edge of the pane of glass by the latch was cracked, the putty holding it in place dried and breaking away in chunks.

"One more crack won't be noticed," Tim declared and, picking up a pointed stone from beneath the buddleia, screwed his eyes tight and gently tapped at the point where the crack met the frame. In less than a minute, there was a hole in the glass big enough for him to get his index finger through. Taking care not to cut himself, he pushed his finger through and flicked the latch handle over on itself.

"Bingo!" he murmured. "Give me a leg up. I'll go inside and open the back door for you."

Pip bit her lip as he eased himself in and disappeared from sight.

The garage was empty except for a large cardboard box containing a replacement for the rotted window through which Tim had just slipped, some gardening tools and a very ancient workbench on to which he lowered himself. Closing the window to cover his tracks, Tim then jumped to the floor, making sure not to step in a covering of white chalk-like dust on the floor: the last thing he wanted to do was to leave footprints. The door into the house was locked, but the mechanism was faulty and a quick jerk opened it.

His heart pounding, Tim stepped into Yoland's house, shutting the door behind him.

He rapidly went down a short passageway to the kitchen and, opening the security lock on the back door, let Pip and Sebastian in.

"Over to you, Sebastian," Tim said. "It's your show from here on. Where do we start?"

"It is my considered opinion," Sebastian replied, "we might be well advised to commence in the room in which the closed curtains preclude the entry of day-light."

"And in English we say?" Tim replied sarcastically.

Opening the door of what must have been the second bedroom, they stepped in. Weak daylight filtered through the closed curtains. The room was furnished as a study. A low, two-drawer, gray metal filing-cabinet stood against a wall, to one side of which was pinned a cork noticeboard. The papers attached to it concerned school matters and were neatly arranged to overlap each other. Cautiously, Tim tested one of the cabinet drawers. It was unlocked.

"What does it contain?" Sebastian inquired.

Tim quickly thumbed through the folders. They contained past examination papers, teaching notes for chemical experiments, staff-meeting agendas, teaching-union information, past pupil records, government education directives and local-education-authority circulars.

"Nothing," Tim replied at length. "Just school junk."

Opposite the filing cabinet was an old-fashioned wooden office desk on top of which stood a brand-new computer, a fourteen-inch TFT screen, a compact laser printer and a scanner. Before the desk was a new typist's chair.

"*Ay caramba!*" Tim exclaimed admiringly. "Now that's a piece of gear! You two do the rest of the joint while I boot this baby up!"

It took Sebastian and Pip very little time to cover the

rest of the bungalow. The bedroom was plain, no suit-cases under the bed that needed investigation, only a few clothes in the wardrobe. All the drawers were half empty. In the kitchen, there was very little food, the fridge-door shelves holding only a liter of milk, five eggs and a half-used pack of butter. The only loaf in the bread bin had a fine coating of mold upon it.

"He must eat out most of the time," Pip said.

"He has no urgent need to eat," Sebastian rejoined. "As do not I."

"You mean you don't eat!"

"I eat the food your mother kindly offers me, but nothing else. It is more than sufficient."

"Hibernating animals build up fat supplies in their bodies," Pip said. "I suppose you do the same."

"No," Sebastian answered. "If you recall, my father's potion, *aqua soporiferum*, not only induces sleep but slows the functions of the body. This, in turn, reduces the need for nourishment."

"So, whatever Yoland uses, does the same?"

"To some extent. His elixir is not as efficient as my father's potion, hence the presence in the kitchen of some comestibles — I mean —" Sebastian interrupted himself "— foodstuffs."

Pip smiled and said, "Better. But just say food."

They moved on. The lounge was as sparse as the kitchen, the dining room likewise. Even in the bath-room were only the basics for bodily hygiene — a sponge, a bar of coal-tar soap, a bottle of two-in-one shampoo and conditioner, a toothbrush, a tube of tooth-paste, a razor and a bottle of shaving foam.

When they returned to the study, it was to find Tim leaning back in the typist's chair.

"It's password protected," he said gloomily. "I've tried to break it, but . . ." He held up his hands in surrender.

Sebastian looked over Tim's shoulder. The cursor was blinking and an on-screen message requested the administrator's password.

"Try *astromel*," Sebastian suggested.

"What does it mean?" Pip asked as Tim entered it and pressed *return*.

"It is an ancient French word, frequently used in spells by Gerbert d'Aurillac," Sebastian explained. "It may be that Yoland, feeling himself secure in the twenty-first century, might use such words unknown today."

The words *Incorrect log-on. Please check user name and password* came up on the screen.

"No go!" Tim said.

"In that case," Sebastian said, "try *ablanathanalba*."

"*Abla*-what?" Tim retorted. "Bit of a mouthful, isn't it?"

"I shall spell it for you," Sebastian said. "It is an ancient word dating to the time of Our Lord and most commonly used in my father's day."

"What does it mean?" Pip wanted to know.

"Of that it is best you remain ignorant," Sebastian said and he spelled it out.

Tim keyed it in. When he pressed *return*, the screen went directly to the Microsoft Windows desktop.

"Open sesame!" he muttered gleefully. "How much time have we got, sis?"

"Twenty minutes," Pip answered.

Tim concentrated on Yoland's directories, going through them as fast as he could. There were over a hundred of them, each with up to twenty sub-directories. Some dealt with school matters but most concerned abstruse scientific data, predominantly nuclear physics and chemistry. They were not only written in English, but in other European languages, Chinese and Japanese.

"There's no way I can ever download all this in twenty minutes," he commented. "And if I did, I wouldn't understand a word of it."

"What about the Internet?" Pip suggested. "Have a look at his *Favorites* folder."

"Good one, sis!" Tim replied. "Girl meets Techno Age."

"You really can be full of yourself sometimes, Tim," she came back, peeved.

Tim clicked on Yoland's Web browser. There were more than two hundred sites listed.

"Sorry, sis," he apologized. "Switch the printer on."

"Sure you think I know how?" Pip said as she depressed the power button.

Nothing happened. Pip knelt down. The printer was disconnected from the wall socket. She crawled under the desk, pushing the plug into the socket. The printer whirred. Tim clicked the mouse and the printer sucked in the first sheet of paper.

"Look at this!" Pip called up, her head still under the desk. "There's more down here than an electricity socket."

Sebastian and Tim peered beneath the desk. Next to the socket was an old, much-battered and scratched, brown leather attaché case with tarnished brass buckles.

Beside that, set into the wall, was a small safe with a combination lock.

"We're going to need more than some magic word to pry that open," Pip declared.

"Stick of gelignite, more like," Tim replied.

"Gelignite?" Sebastian asked.

"Explosive, gunpowder."

"Ah!" Sebastian exclaimed. "Of this I have heard. Roger Bacon, a monk and alchemist before my father's time learned of it from the Orient. In the reign of the Virgin Queen, there were factories creating it, the science taught by a German monk called Berthold Schwarz."

"Never mind the history lecture," Pip said tartly. "What are we going to do about it?"

Squirming under the desk, Tim despondently spun the combination lock's dial. It ticked like a frenetic clock as the tumblers inside rose and fell — then he had an idea.

"When you knew Yoland," Tim said, "like when you were a boy, he was about thirty years old. Right? And let's say you were about ten. Right?"

"That would be approximately correct."

"And you were born in 1430. So, in 1440, Yoland was about thirty. Therefore he was born around 1410."

"Yes . . ."

"What has this to do with the price of eggs?" Pip asked.

Tim did not reply but started to revolve the combination lock this way and that.

"1410 . . . 1409 . . . 1408 . . . 1407 . . ." he began to recite aloud. At 1406, he stopped and, looking up at

Sebastian, said, "Yoland was thirty-four when you knew him."

The other two bent down. The safe was open.

"How did you . . . ?" Pip began.

"Easy. Like all scientists, Yoland's a man of method. We have to lock our school lockers with a number that is an important year. As he said, like our year of birth. What could be more important than that? So . . ."

"*Quod erat demonstrandum*," said Sebastian. "In English," he added, looking Tim straight in the eye, "you say 'That which was to be demonstrated,' which implies it has now been achieved with ease."

Tim winked and started to remove a number of small boxes the size of paperback books from the safe, passing them to Pip, who placed them on the desk. Sebastian opened them.

The first contained gold jewelry and five modern gold sovereigns. Yet none was complete. The jewelry had been cut up with pliers, and several slices had been clipped out of the gold coins. The second box was filled with silver jewelry, similarly defaced, while in the third was a large platinum and diamond brooch, with most of the stones removed and the precious metal cut into roughly equal pieces.

"Look at those," Pip remarked, pushing the diamonds around the box with her finger. "Aren't they gorgeous?"

"Girl's best friend," Tim replied and he ducked down for the remaining box in the safe.

Although it was the same size as the others, the fourth box was heavier. Tim had to reverse out from under the desk to hand it to Sebastian. He put it next to the others and opened it. Within were at least a dozen spell keys, each wrapped in tissue paper.

"He's made these from the jewelry and coins," Tim said.

"Indeed he has," Sebastian agreed as he counted the spell keys, "and he is yet to fashion more. There are but thirteen here. As each spell requires four, he has to make them in multiples of four."

"So he has to make sixteen in all," Pip said.

"Or twenty . . ." Sebastian added.

". . . or twenty-four, or twenty-eight," Tim went on.

Beside the spell keys in the box were several dozen ancient gold coins, each in a plastic money envelope.

"What are these?" Tim exclaimed, slipping one out of its envelope and onto the palm of his hand.

It did not shine like modern gold, with a garish brightness, but with a rich luster. On one side was depicted a kingly figure standing in a ship holding a sword and shield: the reverse bore a cross, four crowns and four crowned lions.

"They are gold nobles," Sebastian said. "I have made mention of them to you. They were currency in my father's time. These are from the reign of King Henry the Sixth."

"How much is it worth?" Tim asked as he went to replace the coin in the plastic envelope and return it to the box. Yet he could not. It seemed stuck to his skin.

"I can't let go of it," he said with alarm.

"It is attracted to you," Sebastian stated, "and you to it. This is Yoland's intention, that whosoever handles the coins shall be entranced by them. Being pure gold, it has captivated you, it has stolen your heart as a lover might. I shall remove it."

With that, Sebastian muttered a few words, pried the coin away from Tim's hand and, slipping it into the plastic envelope, put it back in the box.

"How did you do that," Pip inquired, "when Tim couldn't?"

"I have no interest in gold," Sebastian replied, "and informed the coin of this fact. The spell, as it were, was momentarily cast asunder."

"Neither have I an interest . . ." Tim said.

"You think you have not," Sebastian cut in, "but did you not ask me its value?"

"It's a fair question," Tim admitted, smiling guiltily. "I was wondering what I could buy with it."

He bent down to return the box to the safe with the others, making sure he put them back in the same order as he had found them. As his face passed the level of the desk top, his eye caught the lower right-hand corner of the computer monitor.

"Criperooney!" he almost yelled. "It's six minutes past five!"

Closing the safe, Tim spun the combination wheel. At that moment, the printer stopped. He switched off the socket, yanking the plug out. Sitting in the typist's chair, he shut down the computer, the hard disk droning to a standstill. Removing the printouts from the output tray, he folded them over and put them in his shirt.

"Are we ready?" he asked.

"Chair wheels," Pip said.

Tim looked down. The rollers on the chair legs had, under Yoland's weight, made dents in the carpet. Tim moved the chair so they fitted into them.

"Right!" he said, making certain the keyboard was in the exact position in which he had found it. "Let's beat it!"

They turned for the door. Pip gasped. The floor was heaving with massive cockroaches over five centimeters in length, their sinuous feelers stretching out and quivering, testing the air for vibrations. Their backs shone as if they were made of polished mahogany. Despite their numbers, they made no sound whatsoever.

Pip squeaked involuntarily. At the sound, the antennae stopped wavering, swung in her direction and began to tremble.

Even as they watched, the cockroach cohorts swelled. In seconds, they stood four or five deep, balanced on each other's carapaces. They were like the phalanx of a grotesque miniature army. Now they began making a soft scrambling noise as they fought to keep a foothold on the one below.

"What are we going to do?" whispered Pip, her voice unsteady, her hands shaking and her face white.

"Move slowly to the window," said Tim.

"No!" Sebastian ordered. "If we go out by the window, we will not be able to close it behind us and Yoland will know someone has been here. We must leave through a door."

The cockroach army began to advance, those on top falling forward to be engulfed by those below. It was as if a vile, brown, living wave was rolling over the floor engulfing everything in its path.

Tim shrugged.

The cockroaches tipped their grotesque heads to one side in unison at his movement.

"Nothing we can do," Tim said resignedly and, taking two steps back, ran full tilt at the insects.

As one, the insects took to the wing, a solid cloud flying at him, thudding into him, striking him in the face. The smallest tried to infiltrate his ears and nostrils. The air filled with the insane hiss and rustle of their wings. Tim swatted them against his shirt and blazer, slapping at his cheeks to dislodge them. He grabbed at them with his hands, squeezing fistfuls of them, feeling the creamy, viscous pulp of their intestines slick against his skin.

Pip screamed and followed him. Cockroaches beat into her face, landing on her hair, scrabbling down it, seeking a way to squirm and scratch themselves into her clothing. Their legs were sharp with spines. She could feel them scratching and itching on her back, down her chest and, scraping lower, towards her stomach. Her mouth closed against them, she thrashed her hands across in front of her eyes to try to get through the obscene tempest.

The corridor filled with a sibilant blizzard of cockroaches. Tim stumbled towards the vague outline of the front door and the square of daylight shining through the glass panel, sepia-colored from the fog of cockroaches.

Sebastian followed Pip, lashing the air with his arms,

his hands spread like paddles with which to bat the cockroaches down.

At last they reached the front door. Tim fumbled with the latch and finally tripped it, tugging the door inward. Behind it, a wedge of trapped cockroaches battered themselves against the glass and, landing on the wall, scurried across it, making for the cover of the back of a mirror hanging over an umbrella stand.

Tim stumbled out into the front garden, staggering towards the gate. Behind him came Pip and Sebastian, their clothing smeared with cockroach entrails. Pip's hair was festooned with brown wing-cases and sections of polished brown thorax. The live cockroaches clinging to them dropped to the ground and scuttled back into the bungalow.

"Somebody's going to have to close the front door," said Pip, looking over her shoulder.

"I'll do it," Tim volunteered.

He walked tentatively back down the short path and reached in cautiously for the door handle. Inside, everything looked undisturbed. There was not a sign of even one squashed cockroach although, by the kitchen door, one was squeezing itself into a crack in the wall, carrying a section of a dead comrade.

Tim closed the door, walked to the holly bush, picked up his bag, grinned and said, "Piece of cake!"

"Mum's not going to be happy," Pip rejoined. What're we going to tell her?"

"Cooking class. Pot boiled over," Tim replied.

"We don't take cooking until after vacation."

"And she knows?"

"I don't like lying to Mum," Pip said.

"In that case," Tim answered, "tell her you broke into a teacher's house and got attacked by his pet roaches. Sometimes, a white lie's better than a black truth."

Eight

Lines of Power

A round the chemistry laboratory were arrayed a dozen labeled Pyrex beakers and test tubes containing liquid and accompanied by books of litmus papers or dropper bottles of indicator reagent. The pupils, wearing protective goggles, tested each sample for its degree of alkalinity or acidity. This done, they wrote up the results in their exercise books and then showed them to Yoland.

Pip watched as, one by one, the pupils approached the demonstration bench to hand in their work. Yoland quickly ran through it with a red ballpoint pen, entering a grade in his book and handing the exercise back.

As each pupil returned to their place, Pip noticed that, for the first few steps they took from the demonstration bench, they had a glazed stare in their eyes.

"He's looking into everyone's soul," she whispered to Tim.

He nodded and, picking up his book, gave his work a final check over.

"Take care!" Pip quietly urged as her brother left his stool. "Have you got your clicker . . . ?"

Tim felt in his pocket and nodded.

"So, Ledger," Yoland inquired as Tim approached him, "any problems?"

"None, sir," Tim said, making sure to keep his eyes averted from Yoland's and his hand on the clicker in his pocket.

"And what do you understand by the meaning of pH?"

"It's a scale of zero to fourteen measuring how acidic a liquid is," Tim replied.

"And if something has a pH of seven, what is it?" Yoland continued. "Acidic or otherwise?"

"Seven means . . ." Tim began, but Yoland interrupted him.

"It is polite, young man," the teacher said sharply, "to look someone in the eye when speaking to them."

"Yes, sir," Tim answered then, looking directly into Yoland's face, he went on, "Seven is neutral."

"And a pH of thirteen?"

Tim sensed the master's eyes boring into his own. Something told him the man was buying time in order to complete a probing of his mind. For a moment, Tim wondered if this was how a rabbit might be hypnotized by a stoat or a snake by a mongoose. It took an effort to concentrate on the answer.

"Very alkaline, sir."

"And what color does litmus paper go in an acidic liquid?"

By now, Tim was struggling to hold Yoland at bay. It was as if his eyes could not move from those of the teacher. He tried to direct his thoughts towards something that might allow him to block the stare, prevent Yoland from digging any deeper into him.

The best tactic, he knew from his junior school experience, was to think of vomit. Not just a little splatter on the floor but a plateful of it before him on the table, made up of half-digested baked beans, masticated crinkle-cut fries, chewed-up mushrooms, egg yolk and tomato skins. On the side of the plate was a dollop of chutney and a splodge of brown sauce. With that picture in mind, Tim believed, nothing could get in. He had diverted many a telling-off with such a tactic, turning white enough at the vomity vision to scare the admonishing teacher into sympathy.

Yet despite this, Yoland continued, bit by bit, to edge into his soul. He could feel it. It was like the time he and Pip had secretly sampled the contents of their father's liquor cabinet, the warm rum seeping into their veins, the light-headed feeling creeping over them.

"Red," Tim replied vaguely.

He had to break Yoland's grip over him. It was growing stronger the longer he stood there. There was nothing he could do. Feeling for the clicker in his pocket, Tim held it between finger and thumb and squeezed.

Silence.

His handkerchief was snagged on the steel strip.

"Good," Yoland praised him. "And a pH of three?"

Fumbling in his pocket, Tim struggled to get the clicker free.

"Very acidic indeed, sir," he answered, regaining a little control over himself and hoping this might be the end of it.

It was not. Yoland continued to look into Tim's eyes.

"Do you feel all right, boy?" the master inquired,

still looking hard at Tim. "What are you fiddling about in your pocket for?"

"Hankie, sir," Tim replied. "I was feeling a bit queasy. I feel a bit better now."

Still the clicker would not separate from the handkerchief. Tim was feeling desperate. Yoland was peering at him all the harder.

From somewhere in the classroom came an audible click. Yoland immediately looked away from Tim. The hypnotic hold instantaneously faded.

"Who was that?" Yoland asked.

Pip's face appeared over the rim of her workbench as she stood up.

"I dropped my pencil, sir," she replied, holding it so Yoland could see it.

The master made no reply but glanced at Tim's work, pushed his exercise book across the desk and ordered, "Return to your seat and start reading the chapter on the properties of acids." He looked over Tim's head. "Who's next?"

"Thanks, sis," Tim said softly as he reached his seat. "Close call, that one."

"But . . . ?" Pip quietly asked.

"Don't go up. Pretend to keep on working. He tried it on with me," Tim admitted.

"Why didn't you click?" Pip asked.

"I couldn't," Tim whispered back. "Got snared up in my pocket."

"You did not allow him to . . ." Sebastian began.

"No way!" Tim replied. "I concentrated on something else."

"The usual?" Pip inquired.

Tim smirked and, nodding, said, "Up-chuckery. I hope he enjoyed the sight of the technicolor yawn I was imagining."

"Up-chuckery?" Sebastian wondered aloud. "Technicolor yawn?"

"Modern speak," Pip whispered.

"Tell you later," Tim answered. "When we're having our sandwiches."

"How do you breathe down here?" Tim inquired as Sebastian closed the door to his subterranean chamber. "Look at the candles. They don't even flicker so there's no draft, but the air doesn't smell musty. What's more, the candles must use up a lot of oxygen. And," he added, "when they burn down, where do you get replacements from? You can hardly nip down the supermarket . . ."

Sebastian said nothing but smiled knowingly.

"Sebastian," Pip said tentatively. "There is something I want to know. What is it about Rawne Barton, about this area, that attracts such . . . ?" She was not quite sure how to put it. "Well, Malodor and Yoland and . . . well, you."

At this, Sebastian went to the bookshelves and, bringing a leather folder to the table, opened it to produce a map drawn on vellum which crackled as he spread it out.

"This map is of an area of perhaps five leagues' radius from this house," Sebastian explained. "You will observe how certain buildings and locations are indicated but no place names are given."

"Not much use then," Tim said.

"On the contrary," Sebastian replied, "this map is unique."

He took a glass ruler out of a drawer beneath the table top. At least a meter long, it was etched with a strange scale delineated in Arabic and Greek numerals. He laid it across the map.

"Note," Sebastian went on, "how along the line of this measure there are a number of specific places — three churches, an ancient hilltop settlement from before the time of Our Lord, the junction of three ancient ways, a pointed hill, a large house . . ."

"So they're in a line," Tim said.

"They are not *in* a line," Sebastian retorted. "They are *on* a line. It is known as a ley line, along which travels the power of nature." Turning to Tim, he asked, "Do you have a modern map of this region?"

In a few minutes, they were squatting on Pip's bedroom floor, an Ordnance Survey map spread out before them, the glass ruler beside it.

"See here," Sebastian pointed out. "Even today these lines remain. The churches are ancient structures and, like many churches in the countryside, were probably built on pre-Christian religious sites, the settlement is marked as an Iron Age hill fort, one of the roads is designated a Roman road and the house . . ."

"That's Rawne Barton!" Pip exclaimed.

"Yes," Sebastian confirmed.

"And," Tim went on, "that's why the Romans dug a holy well here . . ."

". . . and," Pip presumed, "why your father built . . ."

"Precisely," Sebastian said. "There is more."

He put the glass ruler across the modern map and, taking a pencil from Pip's desk, started to draw other lines. When he was done, eleven ley lines were shown to converge and end on Rawne Barton, many others passing through it.

"We're at the center of the whole shooting match!" Tim exclaimed.

"How far do they go?" Pip asked.

"Some," Sebastian answered, "are but some miles in length. Others may be up to one hundred miles long."

"So this natural power runs along these lines like electricity down a power cable?" Tim asked.

"In a manner of speaking," Sebastian answered.

"And I suppose it's at its most powerful where the lines intersect," Pip said.

"Yes," Sebastian said bluntly.

"You two still up?" Mr. Ledger called through Pip's bedroom door. "It's past eleven. The witching hour is nigh."

"Little does he know," Pip whispered.

"Just finishing off some geography homework, Dad," Tim called back.

"Five minutes," their father replied. "Then hit the sack. It's a school day tomorrow."

146

Nine

The Atom Club

Over the weekend, Pip and Tim were obliged to go away with their parents to stay with their great-aunt Joan who, Tim pointed out to Pip, was definitely not a candidate for the English throne but could still possibly be accused of witchcraft. She owned a sly-faced Persian cat with yellow eyes and her Irish stew tasted as if the recipe — Tim was sure — included larks' toes, snails' ears, and foxes' snouts.

To bolster her brother's suspicion, Pip found a volume among their aunt's cookbooks entitled *Courtly Meals from Courtly Days,* which included instructions for the making of such dishes as *jellie of pyke, conyngys in graueye or with siryppe of honeye, sparwes in aspic* and *trype de motoun.* To kill time until they left, Tim tentatively translated the titles into pike jelly, rabbits in gravy or honey syrup, sparrows in solidified beef stock and the stomach lining of a sheep. Only one, *whyte wortys,* defeated even his wildest guess.

"Bet this little lot would have Sebastian's mouth watering," he declared.

They did not return to Rawne Barton until Sunday

evening. When, on entering the kitchen, Mr. Ledger went to the alarm panel to deactivate the system, he was met by a blinking diode beeping on the control box.

"Something's triggered the alarm while we've been away," he said. "Probably a mouse or a spider on a sensor or something. I'll give the security firm a ring although, if there had been a problem, they'd have called me on my mobile phone." He studied the electronic display. "It was in the sitting room."

"I'll check it," Tim offered, yet no sooner had he done so than he regretted it. His parents always shut or locked all the internal doors before going away. The intruder — or whatever it was — could still be in there, hunched in a corner, undetected by the sensors, motionless, waiting . . .

With trepidation, Tim put his hand on the door handle and gingerly opened it a few centimeters. Through the crack, all seemed in order. He opened it wider.

The sitting room was undisturbed. Even a car magazine he had dropped on the floor by the armchair just before they had left on Saturday remained open at the page he had been reading. He inspected the windows. They had been neither forced nor opened but, on the outside sill of one of them, was a small clod of dried mud with a beech leaf embedded in it.

"Mouse or spider," he confirmed, returning to the kitchen where his mother was beginning to prepare supper.

"Any homework to do?" Mrs. Ledger inquired.

"Did it on Friday," Pip and Tim chorused.

"In that case," she responded as Mr. Ledger went into the sitting room to switch on the television, "supper in fifteen minutes."

Pip and Tim went upstairs. Sebastian was sitting on Pip's bed. He looked drained. His face was pale and his body hunched.

"Are you all right?" she asked anxiously.

Sebastian did not reply. Tim appeared at the door.

"Sis . . ." he began, then he saw Sebastian. "What's happened?"

"I have spent most of your absence defending this house," Sebastian said in a weak voice.

"From what?" Pip asked uneasily.

"From the wodwo," Sebastian answered.

"The wodwo!" Tim exclaimed. "You mean Scrotton's been here?"

"Yes," Sebastian replied. "He spent some hours attempting an entry last night. He was unsuccessful but, while endeavoring to open a window, he caused the alarm to operate."

"Do you think Yoland sent him?" Pip asked.

"It is possible," Sebastian said. "To Yoland, this house has a certain reputation. However, I think his intention was for Scrotton to ascertain if anything out of the ordinary was occurring here. All he saw was a normal family domicile."

"If he had got in," Tim mused aloud, "he would have found my printout of his master's Internet Favorites list . . ."

"How did you keep him out?" Pip asked.

Sebastian smiled knowingly and replied, "There is

more to Frère d'Aurillac's book than Scrotton has discovered. Eventually, some men in uniforms with powerful lights and two large dogs arrived and Scrotton fled."

The sound of footsteps approached Pip's door along the corridor.

"That's our mother," Tim warned. "You'd best hide or she'll want to know how you come to be here only a few minutes after we've got back."

No sooner had he spoken than Mrs. Ledger knocked on the door and inquired, "Can I come in, Pip?"

Pip was about to stall her, but Sebastian had vanished into thin air.

As their mother came in, Tim squeezed by her in the doorway and went to his room to boot up his computer. It was as he waited for it to get up and running that he noticed the window and his spine crept. On the outside, the glass was smeared with dried streaks of mud. It was plain they had been made by hands scrambling to get in.

It was Sebastian who first saw the announcement. Written in Yoland's immaculate handwriting, it was pinned to the science department noticeboard and read:

The Atom Club

*Starting on Monday, the Atom Club will meet every week
at lunchtime in Chemistry Lab One.
Membership restricted to Years Seven and Eight.
Keen on Science?
Come and join!
More wonders of Science than you'll ever see in lessons.*

"What do you make of that?" Tim pondered.

Sebastian considered the notice before replying, "I cannot say, yet I sense it is ill-omened."

"Whatever the case," Pip said, "we've no option but to join."

And so it was that, the following Monday, the twelve founding members of the Atom Club, including Pip, Tim and Sebastian — and Scrotton — sat on stools in a semicircle in front of the demonstration bench. Behind it stood Yoland, a complex molecular model made of large colored beads and rods at his side.

"Scientists," he began, "know that radioactive elements have what is called a half-life. This is the length of time it takes for their radioactivity to decay by half. It is like saying you have a kilo of sugar but every hour it grows less by fifty percent. After an hour, you have only 500 grams left, another hour 250, another hour 125 and so on."

"What happens when there's nothing left, sir?" Pip asked.

"A good question," Yoland replied. "In the process of decay, the element changes into another form of itself or, possibly, into another element. For example, when uranium-238 decays, it forms thorium-234. It follows, therefore, that there is never nothing left."

"How long does it take?" asked another pupil.

"It varies," Yoland answered. "The isotope of carbon-14 has a half-life of 5,730 years, but uranium-238 has a half-life of four and a half billion years."

"What's an isotope?" questioned someone.

"An isotope is another form of an element," Yoland replied.

"Are there any that have short half-lives?" Tim inquired.

"Indeed, there are," Yoland responded. "Some elements have exceptionally short half-lives. Rubidium-94 has a half-life of just under three seconds. Now," he glanced up at the laboratory clock, "the bell will ring soon so let us move on to a practical demonstration before we cease for today."

At this point, Yoland reached along the demonstration bench and pulled over a piece of equipment that reminded Tim of a car-battery charger. It had several switches on the front, a dial and a wire leading to a sensor that looked like an aluminium cigar tube.

"This," Yoland announced, "is a Geiger counter. It measures the presence of radioactivity." He flicked a switch. A small red light came on. "As you can see," he announced, waving the sensor about in the air, "we are in this classroom virtually devoid of radioactivity. There is in existence what is called background radiation, given off by the ground or substances in it. Granite, for example, emits such radiation in measurable quantities but otherwise we are comparatively free of it. However . . ." He cast a look at Scrotton. "Will you do the honors, Scrotton?"

Without a word, Scrotton entered the preparation room and reappeared carrying a large polished steel canister. On the side was painted the bright yellow and black propeller-like warning sign for radioactive material. From the way he moved, it was obviously very heavy, but he had no difficulty lifting it on to the bench.

"This container," Yoland explained, "is lined with lead. Radioactivity cannot usually penetrate this metal and so it acts as a protective shield." He moved it to the middle of the bench. "In this is a radioactive element," he went on. "All radioactivity is dangerous and so must be treated with respect. As the saying goes concerning fire, radioactivity is also a good servant but a bad master."

"Bit like Scrotton," Tim muttered under his breath.

"The element in this container is polonium-212. It is commonly to be found in hospitals where it is used in treating cancer. Radioactivity destroys living cells."

"Can we see it?" asked a boy at the end of the bench.

"No, you may not!" Yoland replied brusquely. "That would be dangerous."

"How big is it?" asked a girl next to him.

"The piece is the size of about six grains of salt," Yoland answered, "and is contained in a block of clear plastic."

"Why?" inquired a second boy.

"Because," Yoland explained, "that way it cannot be lost. Consider how easy it would be to lose a grain of salt."

"What would happen . . . ?" the boy persevered, but Yoland interrupted him.

"The school — at least, this building — would have to be closed down and the NRPB — that's the National Radiological Protection Board — would have to be called in to sweep the building to find it. So," he added, smiling benevolently, "don't get any ideas, any of you. It's stowed away in the chemistry department safe. And there it will remain."

And I bet I know the combination, Tim thought, making sure he was not looking in Yoland's direction as he did so.

"Now," Yoland continued, "all of you step back from the bench. Remove the lid, Scrotton."

Scrotton grasped the canister and slowly unscrewed the lid. Yoland held the cigar-tube sensor over the mouth. Scrotton quickly removed the lid. Immediately, the Geiger counter started clicking furiously, the needle on the dial dancing to and fro. Yoland moved the sensor nearer to the canister until the clicking was an almost continuous high-pitched buzz.

"Replace the lid, Scrotton."

Scrotton did so. Immediately, the Geiger counter fell silent.

"Thus," said Yoland, "are you introduced to the wonders of nuclear energy. For radioactivity is energy. It is what powers the sun, drives the universe, is at the very center of creation."

The bell sounded for the end of the lunch break and the first meeting of the Atom Club broke up.

Sebastian did not speak as they made their way to the first class of the afternoon.

"Something troubling you?" Tim asked as they lined up for the next lesson.

Still, Sebastian kept his peace.

The weak autumn evening sunlight had moved on from the fields of Rawne Barton. The sunset had been a glorious display of orange and scarlet against which the trees by the river had been starkly outlined, as if etched upon the sky in Indian ink. Now, the light was fading fast, the shadows waning into twilight.

Tim sat at his computer, maneuvering a Y-shaped space fighter across the galaxy, avoiding enemy craft, asteroids and deep-space mines that looked like magnified pollen. His craft had already suffered some battle damage and he had to get to the mother ship off Starion 4 before his fuel pile was depleted. His mission was not helped by the fact that one of the rubber suckers on the base of his joystick no longer sucked.

The mother ship had just come into sight as a small dot of light far ahead in cyberspace when Tim's bedroom door abruptly opened and Pip rushed in.

"You'll never learn to knock, will you, sis?" Tim remarked caustically, glancing over his shoulder.

"Never mind knocking!" Pip retorted, stepping towards the window. "Switch off the monitor. Quick!"

"Why?"

"Because we don't want to be silhouetted by it and . . ." She became exasperated. "Just do it!"

Tim pressed the switch. The screen went dead, the room falling into semi-darkness.

"Now look at this!"

Tim joined his sister at the window.

"What?" he said, his eyes not yet adjusted from intergalactic night to earth light.

"Down by the river bank. Can you see anything?"

Tim squinted. The river reflected the last of the sunset.

"Trees, grass, a crow flying . . ." Something on the river bank moved. "A sheep."

"That's no sheep," Pip replied succinctly. "Sheep wander about."

"Well, that one's not exactly doing the marathon."

Yet no sooner had the words left his mouth than the shape darted for cover behind one of the oak trees.

"What the hell was that?" Tim exclaimed.

"That was the fifth one. There's two more behind that oak and another two behind the chestnut tree to the left."

"Get Sebastian!" Tim ordered.

They ran into Pip's room. Tim kept watch at the window as she tapped on the panel. There was no response. She knocked again, harder. Still, there was no sound of Sebastian coming up the tunnel. She tapped harder. Nothing.

"He's not there," she said with alarm.

"Good time to take a hike," Tim retorted. "What do we do?"

He glanced out of the window. In the twilight, six dark, formless shapes began making their way in a line towards the house. They kept low, almost creeping through the grass.

"Do we tell Dad . . . ?" Pip began.

"Tell him what? Dad, there's an army of ghoulies about to attack the house. We'll never hear the end of it. The laughter'll echo for weeks."

"We might not live to tell the tale," Pip replied.

"Besides," Tim added, ignoring his sister's melodramatic remark, "what could he do that we can't? Invite them in for a cup of coffee or a beer?"

Outside, the line was already only fifty meters from the ha-ha. Tim screwed his eyes up and concentrated on what appeared to be the leader, a form slightly ahead of the others.

"It's Scrotton!" he exclaimed then, after a pause, added, "No, it's not — it's *six* Scrottons! He's been replicated!"

Pip felt weak at the knees, her palms began to sweat and her flesh crept.

"If Sebastian's not here . . ." she started, but she was interrupted.

"Look!" Tim blurted out.

As he spoke, a lone figure rose out of the ha-ha and gradually advanced towards the line. It moved slowly, an obvious deliberation in its every action.

"It must be Seb . . ." Tim muttered.

At the figure's appearance, the line of Scrottons became agitated. They started to hop from side to side, jumping up and down with a frenetic flailing of their arms. It was now Tim noticed that they each carried a stout wooden staff.

"He doesn't stand a chance," Pip murmured. "Six to one and they've got weapons."

"No choice then," Tim decided. "Get your shoes on."

"Just going for a walk," he said to their mother as they went through the kitchen.

"Don't be long," she replied, looking up from her ironing, "and be careful. It's getting dark. Don't go down to the river. You might fall in."

Pausing in the garage to let their eyes adjust to the darkness, Tim armed himself with a hedging hook, the curving blade bright where his father had recently sharpened it. Pip found herself an old rusty pitchfork.

They hurriedly tiptoed to the field gate, crouched down, opened it and edged into the field. Off to the left, the line of Scrottons had halted in a semicircle, Sebastian in the center. Every Scrotton was swinging its club, uttering an obscene noise, like mating frogs in a springtime pond.

"What now?" Tim wondered. "Do we charge them?"

At that moment, Sebastian started to gradually advance. The Scrottons began snarling under their breath and grew more agitated.

"Let's go for it," Tim whispered. "We've at least got the element of surprise."

He stood up, weighed the hedging hook in his hand and set off running at the Scrottons as hard as he could go. Pip was only a few steps behind him.

The line of Scrottons swung around with military precision to face them, halted as if gathering their strength, then came at them. For a moment, Tim faltered, but both he and Pip knew they had gone past the point of no return. They were committed to battle.

In seconds, the first Scrotton was almost upon them. Tim lashed at it with the hedging hook but missed. It ran on by, heading for Pip. She rammed the handle of the pitchfork into the ground before her, angling it at her adversary. Under its own momentum, the Scrotton ran on to the pitchfork, the prongs going deep into its chest. Blood spurted on to Pip's clothing. She screamed. The wodwo hissed like an angry lizard, thrashing to and fro on the pitchfork, wrenching it out of the ground and trying to extract it from its torso.

In the meantime, Tim had a second Scrotton lunge at him. He swung the hedging hook at it, feeling it shudder as the metal blade sunk into its shoulder, striking bone. The Scrotton grunted, jerked the tool out of Tim's hands, twirled it in mid-air with as much ease as a majorette might her baton and lifted it high over his head.

Tim watched as the hook rose as if in slow motion, the sharp sickle-edged blade turning towards him. He tried to dodge, but his feet seemed cemented to the spot. He raised his hands to defend himself or deflect the blow, remembering as he did so seeing his father cut through saplings thicker than dining-table legs with one swipe. His mouth opened to yell, yet no sound came.

The Scrotton in front of Pip finally levered the pitchfork from its chest. Holding it like a javelin, the creature faced Pip and drew its arm back.

The hedging hook fell into the grass at Tim's side. The Scrotton stood not a meter from him. It grunted incomprehensibly and then sank to its knees. Gradually, it seemed to deflate. The Scrotton before Pip was also collapsing as if punctured. Elsewhere, three of the other Scrottons were similarly shrinking, yet one was not. It stood its ground before Sebastian, glaring at him, its eyes like small glowing coals, bright one moment, dull the next.

Pip and Tim picked up their weapons and rushed to Sebastian's side.

"Behold," Sebastian announced, standing with his legs astride and his arms akimbo, "the wodwo in all its evil panoply."

Before them stood Scrotton, besmirched with mud, his face shining with sweat, his hair matted with twigs and dead leaves.

"You gonna wish you 'adn't messed with me," he threatened, his eyes fixed on Tim, his lip curling like that of an irate dog.

Sebastian made no response. Instead, he raised his left hand. Beneath it, there appeared a cone of blackness darker than the darkest, starless night.

At the sight of it, Scrotton gave a sickening, penetrating squeak, like a rat held in a trap by one leg or its tail. Sebastian stepped across to him so that Scrotton was completely covered by the dark cone. He spun around to escape, but it enveloped him.

"Pip," Sebastian ordered. "Take my right hand and, while holding it, touch Scrotton's head. Yet do not entirely enter the blackness yourself."

Pip did as she was asked but, as her fingers touched Scrotton's hair, she was disgusted and withdrew it.

"Do not flinch," Sebastian said. "He can harm you not."

Steeling herself, Pip closed her eyes and pushed her fingers into Scrotton's filthy hair. She could feel the grease and sweat between her fingers, slick like sun-warmed olive oil.

"Hold still," Sebastian ordered.

A sudden surge of power flooded from Sebastian's hand through Pip's arms. It was as if an electric current were pulling her muscles tight, flexing her tendons. Scrotton started to convulse beneath her touch.

"Together, our strengths combined shall overcome," Sebastian whispered.

In a matter of seconds, he let Pip's hand go. Instantly, the flow of power ceased, and Scrotton collapsed as if his skeleton had suddenly been removed from his body.

"What do we do with him?" Tim asked. "We can't leave him here."

"He will, like any creature," Sebastian replied as Pip wiped her hand clean on the grass that was already damp with dew, "find his way to his burrow."

With Tim carrying the hedging hook and pitchfork, the three of them returned to the house. By chance, Mrs. Ledger had joined her husband in the living room.

Slipping past the door undetected, they went upstairs where, once in her room, Pip changed and put her bloodstained clothing in cold water to soak. The bloodstains, she noticed, were very weak, as if the blood had been diluted. When she was done, hiding the basin under her bed, Sebastian and Tim joined her.

"Well, we've blown it!" Tim exclaimed ruefully to Sebastian. "Now Yoland'll know you're in cahoots with us and that we've rumbled his familiar."

"On the contrary," Sebastian replied. "Scrotton will remember nothing of tonight."

"Like, yes!" Tim replied. "We've just trounced his army of darkness."

"Like yes, indeed," Sebastian answered, smiling. "I have erased his short-term memory. His brain is not a complex organ. It was a simple process."

"The other five Scrottons . . ." Pip ventured timorously. "They weren't homunculi . . . ?"

At this, Sebastian's smiled faded.

"Only in a manner of speaking. They were in fact merely automatons, replicas with no independent will of their own. They were created for the sole function of fighting on this one occasion."

"Who made them?" Pip asked fearfully.

"I know of only one who has perfected the art thus far . . ." Sebastian replied.

"Malodor," Tim cut in.

Ten

Gathering Clouds

For an hour, Tim sat at his desk with his bedroom door locked and surfed the Internet, logging on to genealogical and census databases, searching parish records, scouring cathedral and university records, and combing library and museum sites. Finally, at ten o'clock, he emerged and, holding a sheet of neatly printed A4, knocked on Pip's door, waited a few moments and went in. She was sitting at her dressing table in her dressing gown, trying out different hairstyles with a set of soft curlers.

"Now that's progress," she congratulated him. "You knocked."

Tim held up the sheet of paper.

"Call up the man!" he commanded.

When Sebastian surfaced from the panel, Tim said, "I've done a bit of digging into Yoland's past." He sat on Pip's bedroom chair just after she whisked her clothes off it.

"It seems," he began, reading from the paper, "that Yoland — or someone with his name — has lived in this area for generations. But," he continued, "there's something strange going on. For long stretches of time, there's no mention of him in the records — then he pops up again. For example, there is no sign of any Yoland between 1450 and 1661; then a Yoland reappears employed as an apothecary. And then, with the exception of 1665, he disappears until a period from 1682 to 1700."

"You have acquired this knowledge through your computer?" Sebastian asked.

"That and the aid of Google," Tim answered.

"Google?" Sebastian repeated.

"A search engine. It helps you to find knowledge anywhere on the Internet. But it still took a bit of serious surfing."

"Surfing?" Sebastian asked.

"Surfing the net, riding the cyber-waves. You'll get it in time."

"Remarkable!" Sebastian said, in obvious awe.

Tim turned his attention back to the printout. "In 1703, Yoland was listed for six years as a watchmaker. Nothing after that until 1899 when he pops up as a jeweler with a shop in Brampton. He enlisted in the Great War in 1914 and was killed in the trenches. From 1939 to 1942, he is listed as the manager of the Brampton Dispensary. He died when a German bomber crashed on the building. In the modern day, he's easy to trace. Our man was born on the 30th of April 1949 in Brampton. You can guess the address on his birth certificate — 14 Peelings Lane. His name is given as Brian Alan Yoland. His mother's name was Margaret Yoland, but his father's name was left blank."

"Perhaps his mother wasn't married," Pip suggested.

"She was married," Sebastian softly announced, adding, "in a manner of speaking."

"What do you mean?" Pip asked.

"Her husband was not of the flesh," Sebastian replied.

"Not of the flesh . . . ?" Pip said, but, having asked the question, she did not want to hear the answer.

"Bride of Frankenstein," Tim said in a deep voice, "starring Boris Karloff." He put his fingers under his eyes, grotesquely pulling his lower eyelids down.

"Shut up, Tim!" Pip said sharply. "What do you mean?"

"All the Yolands through the centuries have been born of woman," Sebastian explained, "but sired by those who are otherwise."

"Otherwise?" Pip inquired.

"Suffice to say Yoland's mother — all the Yolands' mothers — would not have known," Sebastian replied. "They would merely have discovered one day that they were with child."

"Then how on earth . . . ? You know," Tim said, embarrassed by the direction the conversation was taking.

"Shall we just say by magic?" Sebastian replied evasively. "Black magic. Continue with your findings, Tim."

Regaining his composure, Tim went on reading from the printout.

"After primary school, he went to the grammar school that was closed down when Bourne End Comp. was set up. Leaving the grammar school, he went to Merton College, Oxford, where he studied chemistry.

But! Wait for this! When he was an undergraduate student, he wrote a thesis entitled *The Chemistry of Alchemy in the Fifteenth Century*. After getting his degree, he again disappeared but turned up two and a half years later in 1974 as an assistant professor at his old school. He transferred to the comp. when the grammar school closed. He was promoted to head of chemistry in 1982 when the previous head of department was killed by an avalanche while supervising a school skiing trip to Austria. He has never married — and that's it."

Taking the printout from Tim's hand, Pip observed, "Every job a Yoland has had, right up to our Yoland, was either as a jeweler or a chemist."

"In other words, something to do with chemistry or precious metals," Tim replied. "The stuff of alchemy."

"It is not *a* Yoland," Sebastian announced quietly. "It it *the same* Yoland through time. Each baby contains the one soul, the one man within."

"You mean," Pip suggested, "the soul is sort of recycled, and so there aren't generations of Yolands, just the one."

"Precisely," Sebastian confirmed, "and the dates of his appearances are significant. In 1665, it was the outbreak of the Great Plague. The end of the seventeenth century brought war with Scotland and great civil unrest in England. In 1703, there was the worst storm for a thousand years during which half of the nation's merchant ships were sunk and thousands drowned or murdered by wreckers."

"Wreckers?" Tim cut in.

"Those who scoured the coast for wrecks," Sebastian

answered, "rescuing and then killing survivors for their ships' cargoes. They were brutal times. In 1914," he continued, "was the commencement of what you call the Great War. In 1939, the Second World War began."

"You don't mean Yoland's played a part in all of this?" Pip asked, incredulously.

"No," Sebastian answered. "Were that the case, I should have awoken every time and yet I did not. However, it is greatly coincidental that he was present."

"Don't you only wake up if de Loudéac's around the place?" Tim asked. "You said . . ."

"Yes, that is generally true. Yet great evil may stir me."

"So Yoland's not necessarily the reason . . ." Pip began.

". . . and you've woken up now," Tim said, finishing his sister's sentence.

"Yes," Sebastian replied pensively, "I have, have I not . . . ?"

"So when Yoland was around," Tim wanted to know, "what was he doing?"

"I believe," Sebastian responded, "he was researching, studying the ways of men or women at their very worst."

"And now you think he's come to put his knowledge to use?"

Sebastian looked from Pip to Tim and back again.

"It is my considered opinion," Sebastian said slowly, "that Yoland has been preparing a long time for what he now plans."

". . . which is?" Tim asked.

Sebastian made no answer.

The following day, as they left the chemistry laboratory after registration, Pip felt a hand touch the back of her neck. Fingers quickly ran down her nape, blunt, thick nails scrambling at her skin. In less than a second, the chain holding the pendant tightened at her throat and cut into her flesh.

"I'll 'ave this bauble," muttered a voice behind her.

With a sharp tug, Scrotton yanked the chain. It broke. Pip felt the pendant whip over her collarbone. Without breaking his step, Scrotton continued towards the classroom door. Gathering the chain into his hand, he slid it into his pocket.

Tim and Sebastian were ahead of her in a wedge of other pupils, pushing to get out, so there was nothing they could do. Pip took two paces after Scrotton and lashed out at him. The flat of her hand hit his ear and he stumbled. The momentum of her action spun her around, and her bag caught a test-tube rack put out for the next class. It fell to the floor in a shattering of glass, the wooden rack breaking into splinters.

Tim and Sebastian, with everyone else, stopped in their tracks and looked around. No one spoke. The silence was almost tangible.

"So?" Yoland said menacingly, as he approached Pip.

"I'm sorry, sir," Pip said timidly, staring at her feet.

"My little lecture at the beginning of term seems not to have impressed itself upon you," Yoland remarked acidly.

He bent down and gazed straight into Pip's eyes. She felt him seeking out her soul and fumbled in her pocket for the clicker, pressing the little steel tongue. Yoland immediately withdrew from looking at her, and she sensed his influence wane.

"It did, sir. It was an accident, sir."

Pip knew there was no point in telling him what had really happened. Scrotton would be believed before her: and, for all she knew, Scrotton might have been ordered to steal the pendant. The whole incident might be a setup.

"Accidents do not just happen," Yoland continued through gritted teeth. "They occur through a lack of forethought." He stood up to his full height. "You will go in detention and prepare an essay of at least 300 words on the importance of laboratory safety. In accordance with the school rules, you will either fulfill this penalty after school or during the lunch hour. The choice is yours."

Over by the door, Tim and Sebastian willed Pip to choose the latter option.

"In lunch break, sir," Pip said.

"Yes!" Tim mouthed triumphantly.

"Very well. You will be here at half past twelve precisely," Yoland decreed. "You will have consumed your food before coming."

"Scrotton's stolen the pendant," Pip reported as soon as they were away from the laboratory. "I tried to get it back but . . ."

"It matters not," Sebastian said with a faint smile, "and we may turn this perceived adversity to our advantage. I have noticed that Yoland spends much of his free time around noontide in the preparation room behind the laboratory. Your chastisement will give us an opportunity to observe what it is he employs himself doing."

"But it belonged to Queen Joan," Pip reminded him.

"Be not concerned," Sebastian pacified her. "The pendant can look after itself."

Throughout the midmorning break, Scrotton was nowhere to be seen, only reappearing for math class immediately afterward. He arrived late, just sliding into his seat before the teacher, a gruff woman who wore tweed skirts and heavy shoes, walked into the room.

While worksheets were handed out, Scrotton smirked at Pip, who glowered back at him.

"Pay him no attention," Sebastian advised in a subdued voice. "Concentrate upon your work."

Pip had reached the fourth question on the worksheet when she thought she could just pick up the smell of burning. She glanced around. Tim was concentrating on the work. Sebastian caught her eye and nodded towards Scrotton, who was bent over his desk. From his creased brow and the fact that his tongue protruded from between his lips, Pip guessed he was finding the math exercise very difficult.

As she looked at him, Pip saw something moving by his feet. She glanced down. Scrotton's left shoe was on fire. Tiny flames flickered along the edge of the sole, gradually spreading up the leather towards the bottom of his trousers. The class started to giggle.

"What's going on?" the teacher inquired, turning from the whiteboard upon which she was writing the worksheet answers. She sniffed the air. "Do I detect burning?"

"It's Scrotton, miss," a girl sitting near the back of the room called out, hardly able to contain her laughter. "He's on fire."

By now, flames were licking up Scrotton's pants legs while he tried frantically to beat them out. With every blow at the flames, eddies of smoke puffed out of his jacket cuffs.

Without a moment's hesitation, the math teacher availed herself of a fire extinguisher that hung by her desk, removed the safety pin and, pointing the nozzle squarely at Scrotton, said in a loud voice, "Close your eyes and mouth, boy."

Scrotton barely had time to obey before a stream of dense, pressurized white foam hit him, enveloping him from the waist down.

"Now!" the teacher mused, standing in front of Scrotton as the smoke dissipated, "I wonder how that could have happened?"

"I don't know, miss," Scrotton said in a surly voice.

"I do!" the teacher replied. "Cigarettes. Matches. You know the school rule on smoking."

Scrotton peered miserably at his feet and his still-smoldering shoe.

"On your hind legs!" She addressed the remainder of the class. "You keep quiet and get on with your work. A prefect'll be in shortly to mind you." With that, she led Scrotton out, closing the door behind her. The class fell into a suppressed but agitated chatter.

"How did that happen?" Pip whispered.

"The eye will not be stolen from its owner," Sebastian explained. "If it is, it takes its own revenge upon the thief."

Without leaving his seat, Sebastian leaned over and felt about in the trail of foam Scrotton had made. When he sat up, he had the pendant in his hand. It was still attached to the broken chain.

"I'll get the chain mended," Pip said as Sebastian passed it to her.

"There is no need," Sebastian answered.

He held the two broken ends of the chain between his finger and thumb. When he removed them, the chain was whole once more.

Pip settled down and Yoland, seeing she had begun her punishment, went into the preparation room, closing the door. After a few minutes, Pip heard a faint yet distinct whining noise, reminding her of a wild bees' nest Tim had discovered in a hollow tree at the far end of Rawne's Ground. Standing on the rung of her stool, she was able to peer through the fume cupboard into the preparation room.

Yoland was standing before a condenser reducing and collecting the vapors given off by a brilliant, iridescent blue liquid boiling in a round-bottomed flask poised over a Bunsen burner. Yet there was more than just the liquid in the flask. Small black flies seemed to be hovering in the steam. Then, taking a pipette, he removed a small amount of the distilled liquid from the beaker, running it off into a test tube to which he added a reddish powder. The liquid bubbled as the chemicals mixed. Yoland then gently shook the test tube, mildly heated it over the Bunsen burner and poured the now blood-colored fluid into a petri dish.

Moving slightly to one side, Pip saw on the workbench behind him a large retort held in place over a tripod by means of a silver-painted clamp-stand. As she looked, something black seemed to be moving in the retort, squirming around as though it was uncomfortable in such a confined space. The interior of the retort was misted, as if fogged with condensation. She was reminded of her primary school classroom windows on rainy winter afternoons. Suddenly, pressed against the wall of the retort, was an eye. It was perfectly round, like a bird's, white with a jet black pupil — but it somehow had more to it. A kind of intelligence. And she knew it had seen her. The interior of the retort came alive. Feathers and fur pressed against the glass as if the contents were trying to get out. She briefly saw a beak, a pointed ear and a bright chrome yellow talon like a chicken's foot. Hurriedly, she bobbed down and picked up her pen.

Her punishment hastily finished, Pip took a deep breath to steel herself, approached the preparation room door, ignored the notice, knocked once and went straight in.

"I'm finished, sir," she announced.

Yoland started, quickly placing the test tube in a rack. At the same time, he attempted to position himself between Pip and the petri dish. However, he did not move fast enough to prevent her from noticing that the dish contained one of the gold spell keys. Above it hovered several flies, as large as bluebottles, with shimmering bodies and diaphanous wings. At Pip's arrival they seemed to disappear into the liquid. The retort was nowhere to be seen.

"Put it on the shelf," Yoland said brusquely, "and go. This room is forbidden to pupils."

Pip, glad to get out of the room and Yoland's presence, and mindful of his army of cockroaches, immediately did as she was told, closing the door firmly behind her.

Finding Tim and Sebastian, she recounted what she had seen.

"Do you know what he was doing?" she asked Sebastian.

"He was imbuing the key with the properties he requires it to possess."

"And that must imply," Tim added, "that we're getting near to lift-off."

At the rear of the garage was Mr. Ledger's old mountain bike. As he no longer rode it, Tim asked if Sebastian could have it. Permission granted, he and Pip polished the rust off the wheel rims, oiled the bearings, greased the chain, inflated the tires and called up Sebastian.

"All yours," Tim announced ceremoniously.

Sebastian was taken aback, saying, "This is most generous of you. I am bereft of words to . . ."

Approaching footsteps heralded the arrival of Mr. and Mrs. Ledger.

"So you haven't got a bike after all," Mrs. Ledger remarked.

"Looks good as new," Mr. Ledger said, running his eye over the bike. "Well done, Twin Ledgers. I hope you like it, Sebastian."

"Thank you very much, sir," Sebastian said. "I'm exceedingly grateful to you. I have never owned such a means of locomotion."

Tim winced.

Mr. Ledger smiled and said, "You don't have to address me as *sir*, Sebastian. I'm not one of your teachers. Call me Steve."

"And I'm Sandra," added Mrs. Ledger.

Tim and Pip exchanged glances. Sebastian beamed with pleasure. "I am most touched that you have afforded me such a welcome into your family and I am truly moved by your generosity of spirit."

Tim grimaced and tried to explain Sebastian's vocabulary by saying, "He reads a lot."

"An example you could follow, sunshine!" Mr. Ledger retorted. "Try novels instead of *PC Plus* and *Computer Buyer.*"

When Mr. and Mrs. Ledger returned to the house, Tim and Sebastian set off for a short ride. At first, Sebastian was a little unsteady. He had briefly ridden Mr. Ledger's racing cycle during the summer, when he and Tim had gone into Brampton to search for de Loudéac, but that was his only experience of riding a bicycle. The racer had been lightweight: this one was heavy, and he had to use all twelve gears to keep up with Tim.

By the time they came to cycle home from school

the following afternoon, Sebastian was a steady and confident rider. He did not balk at oncoming traffic: even trucks and white vans which passed very close to him did not faze him in the slightest. Potholes did not unsteady him, he anticipated manholes and drain covers, and he learned to lean over on the corners. He even managed, if only briefly, to ride with his hands off the handlebars.

About half a mile out of the town, they came upon Scrotton heading home to his burrow. He walked quickly, his arms hanging loosely at his side, his head thrust forward. As they overtook him, he sneered at Pip and shouted incomprehensibly after her. Pip waved to him in a friendly manner and smiled. This reaction seemed to enrage Scrotton further. He picked up a pat of dried cow dung from the road and threw it at her. It flew through the air like a frisbee but, by the time he hurled it, Pip was well out of his range, and it soared into the hedge.

Another mile further on, they arrived at the point where the track left the road to head up through the woods towards Scrotton's burrow. Not far past the track, two dead badgers lay on the edge of the tarmac, the grass around their heads thickly puddled with clotted blood, the white stripes on their faces smeared with it and their snouts badly cut. Their hindquarters were pulped where passing cars had run over them.

"At least the roadkills will give the rest of them more space," Pip remarked, saddened by the sight.

"These creatures were not killed by passing vehicles," Sebastian said. "Pay attention to them."

Tim studied the nearest corpse. It had had its throat torn out.

The door into Sebastian's subterranean lair was already open. Through it, Pip and Tim could see the oak table in the center of the chamber, piled high with books. Some were open, others marked with thin slips of colored paper. They ranged in size from a substantial church Bible down to a child's illustrated paperback. Most were bound in leather.

Sebastian neither spoke nor looked up as Pip and Tim entered. He continued to pore over a book with a split spine, the leather flaking into little piles of dust on the polished table. Every now and then he jotted a note on an oblong of parchment using a gold-shafted pen which he periodically dipped in a porcelain inkwell.

Tim sidled over to the bookcases. Upon one shelf, he noticed a number of very modern books. Taking one down, he opened it. It was entitled *Quarks, Quasars and the State of Light*. The author was a professor in an American university. Every page, it seemed, was as full of mathematical equations as it was text.

"Do you understand all this?" Tim asked.

Sebastian's only response was to raise his hand and, without looking up, say, "Indulge me a little longer, Tim, if you will."

Pip crossed the chamber. Sebastian's school jacket was suspended from a hook, incongruous next to his centuries-old homespun cloak. On his bed, the lambs' fleeces under which he slept were in disarray. His pillow sprouted the sharp quill ends of the goose feathers with which it was stuffed.

"I am ready," Sebastian announced at last. "Please join me."

Pip and Tim perched themselves on stools at the table.

"The situation is thus," Sebastian commenced. "Yoland is seeking to disseminate evil through a network of stolen souls. He intends to achieve his aim by the use of a spell from Gerbert d'Aurillac's book, with the assistance of Scrotton and his — the word you use today is *clones*."

"Why is he doing this?" Pip inquired.

"Consider Malodor," Sebastian answered. "He wished to build an automaton that would do his every bidding. Eventually, he would have built more and become a powerful man . . ."

". . . had we not blown his boat out of the water!" Tim interjected.

"With Yoland," Sebastian continued, "the situation is somewhat similar but, instead of creating automata, he wants to turn humans into unquestioning serfs who will obey his command without equivocation."

"What is it with them?" Pip remarked. "This power thing . . . ? I just don't get it."

"Was it not ever thus?" Sebastian observed. "In my father's day, monarchs and noblemen jostled for power. Today, do not presidents and politicians follow likewise? It may be for personal pride or glory, sometimes for personal wealth, but beyond this lies the desire for power for its own sake. However, in Yoland's case, it is more than this. He seeks not just personal power but to further the cause of evil, as might a priest seek to increase the cause of good."

The buttery light from the candles over their heads cast itself upon their faces.

"And you've got to thwart his plan," Tim said.

"He cannot be permitted to succeed," Sebastian stated tersely.

"But what if he does?" Pip ventured.

Sebastian closed the book before him and, looking from Pip to Tim, said, "It bears not thinking about, my friends. What is more," he continued, "I fear I may be unable to arrest his progress. The spells he plans to use are complex, exceedingly efficacious and hazardous. To counteract them may be all but impossible."

"But you can't give up," Pip said. "You've got to give it a go."

"I intend to," Sebastian said sharply, "but I shall need assistance, and there are only two people upon whom I believe I can place my trust implicitly."

"Goes without saying," Pip pledged.

"We joined you in the other one," said Tim. "We'll be there again for you this time. Agreed, sis?"

"Yes," Pip confirmed yet, as she spoke, a quiver of apprehension ran down her spine. That one three-letter word, she considered, had committed her to she dared not imagine what.

"I ask you not to join me unprepared. This time," Sebastian declared, "you will have powers."

"Powers?" Tim echoed.

"Powers," Sebastian confirmed gravely. "This time you will be armed as punitors."

"Armed?" Tim queried eagerly. "Swords, shields, crossbows . . . ?"

"Not exactly," Sebastian said. "A weapon of another sort."

Eleven

To Be a Punitor

"What is a punitor?" Pip inquired.

"The word comes from Latin," Sebastian told her, "and means one who punishes or avenges a wrong."

Sebastian gathered up the books on the table and returned them to the shelves. This done, he placed two highly polished silver-lidded chalices in front of Pip and Tim. They were intricately engraved with runes. He removed the lids, which chimed like minuscule cymbals against the rims.

"I am sure you are familiar with the phrase 'the punishment should fit the crime,'" Sebastian went on. "This you must not forget," he added. "Punitors do not merely punish. They do so justly. They also defend right against wrong."

At this, Sebastian left the table and walked across the chamber to a row of shelves half hidden in shadow. Lifting down a tall-necked flask sealed with a ground-glass stopper, he came back to the table. Directly under the candles, Pip and Tim could see it contained a deep turquoise-colored liquid.

Carefully, Sebastian poured a small draft into each of the chalices.

"I assume becoming a punitor," Pip ventured reluctantly, "involves drinking that?"

"Indeed, no," Sebastian replied. "You must only dampen your lips. If you were to swallow any of the draft . . ."

"You mean it's poisonous?" Tim asked nervously.

"Not precisely . . ." Sebastian answered evasively.

"Apart from that," Tim inquired, "what else . . . ?"

"You must be of good heart," Sebastian declared, "but I consider both of you to be so."

"What if you're not?" Tim pondered anxiously.

A list of his more outrageous transgressions rolled over in his mind, like an autocue in a television studio — the time he poured gin into great-aunt Joan's aquarium tank, sozzling her angelfish; and then at his and Pip's seventh birthday party, he had tied Rebecca Todd's plaits together around the bar on the back of her chair; the occasion on which he telephoned the local pub to say that a car parked outside, numbered R2D2, was flashing its lights and making a beeping noise and the barman had announced the fact to the customers. For the first two, his father had stopped his pocket money for two months and taken away the TV, DVD and video remotes. The telephone call was never traced back to him.

Sebastian laughed quietly and, guessing what was going through Tim's head, said, "You need not worry. Childish misdemeanors will not affect your integrity."

Taking a small bronze rod, Sebastian touched each chalice, which again rang like a tiny bell.

"Are you ready," he inquired, "to bind yourself solemnly and sincerely to the cause of good?"

"Yes," Pip and Tim confirmed in unison.

Sebastian began softly intoning in Latin. Neither Pip nor Tim could pick up more than the occasional mention of their names and a few words the meanings of which they could only hazard a guess — *justicia, diabolus, maligno* . . .

After several minutes, Sebastian fell silent and slid the chalices over the table.

"Remember." Sebastian repeated his warning. "Just wet your lips. Do not then lick them." He placed a square of dark-green silk next to each chalice. "Wipe your mouths dry with these."

Gingerly, they picked up the chalices. As the potion touched their lips, their skin seemed to effervesce as if they had sucked upon a sherbet fizz.

"Weird!" Tim said when he had wiped his mouth dry.

Sebastian picked up the chalices, flinging the contents at the wall. As the liquid hit the stones the chamber was lit by a brilliant light, a shower of orange sparks cascading to the flagstoned floor.

"Wicked!" Tim exclaimed.

"Don't we have to swear an oath or something?" Pip asked.

"Your acceptance of the risk of touching the liquid assures your fidelity," Sebastian answered.

"So now we're punitors?" Tim asked.

Sebastian nodded, picked up the silk napkins and, placing them in a crude earthenware pot, set light to them. They quickly ignited, the cloth spitting and hissing.

"How do we know what powers we have?" Pip inquired. "Is there some way we can test them?"

"That is not necessary," Sebastian answered. "They will become apparent according to what your need is at the time. If you see great evil, your powers will be great. If you see less significant wickedness, your powers will be less, yet still adequate to address it. There is, however, one point you must bear in mind," he ended. "You may avenge evil but you are not protected from it. However, I have prepared tokens which will afford you some protection."

Sebastian handed Pip and Tim each a thin disc of highly polished wood about two centimeters in diameter.

"These are cross-sections of the bough of a rowan tree," Sebastian explained. "They were cut after the tree was dead. One may not fell a living rowan, for to do so is to encourage evil to befall you."

"So what do we do with it?" Pip inquired.

"You merely revolve it in your hand," Sebastian instructed. "So long as you do this, you will reverse any nearby evil. Keep the coin of rowan, with you at all times."

Pip and Tim placed the wooden discs in their pockets.

"So," Tim asked, "how does this punitor power work? Do we have to do something to sort of switch it on?"

"No," Sebastian said. "It will commence just as any emotion might. Consider how you felt when you saw the girl being bullied for her staph infection. You were angry at her antagonist, sympathetic to her. You did not have to switch on these emotions, as you put it. They were automatically aroused in you, for you are good and what you saw was wrong. So will it be. Your powers will come to the fore for they are now extensions of your feelings."

"The Force is with us!" Tim said, punching the air. "We have the power . . ."

"Oh! Tim," Pip said with a weary voice. "Do get a life!"

The following week was vacation. On the Friday before, the entire school was called to assembly before school began, to be addressed by Dr. Singall.

He began his speech by commending the pupils on a solid start to the new school year.

"The soccer season has kicked off particularly well, if you'll excuse my pun," he said with a self-indulgent smile at his own wit, "with not a game lost so far. Our junior boys' cross-country team has won the first round of the inter-county competition. And, lest you think only the boys are faring well, I'm delighted to report that the senior girls' hockey team has scored a resounding victory over Capland Girls' High School."

He continued with a number of announcements concerning the school play, the annual concert, the refurbishment of the Food Technology suite and a forthcoming German exchange in the first week after vacation.

"As those of you going on the German exchange will know," he announced, "you will be accompanied by Mr. Staples and Miss Bates."

This information gave rise to a general murmur and a brief wolf whistle, which were quickly suppressed by a scowl from the headmaster. It was widely known the two teachers were dating each other.

"In their place," Dr. Singall concluded, "we shall have two substitute teachers. Mr. Staples's German classes will be taken by Miss Brandeis and Miss Bates's classes will be taught by Mr. Loudacre."

With that, the school was dismissed to their classes.

Although it was Friday, Yoland let it be known that the Atom Club would meet that lunchtime to make up for the Monday which would be missed over vacation and for the first Monday after vacation which was to be designated an in-service training day. Accordingly, as soon as they had finished their sandwiches, Pip, Tim, and Sebastian made their way to the chemistry laboratory. As they went in, Scrotton was hanging a large color diagram in front of the whiteboard. Once it was up, he lingered at the end of the demonstration bench and surveyed the room.

"Arrogant little runt," Tim whispered. "Thinks he's the man's man."

"Man's monkey, more like," Pip replied under her breath.

"Be sure," Sebastian said softly, his back to Scrotton, "not to underestimate him. He has the ear of his master and, worse, his master has his ear. Even now, he will be monitoring our conversation as best he can."

"Think he can hear us?" Pip asked quietly, her words camouflaged by the general babble in the room.

"It is possible," Sebastian answered, "but we utter nothing of an incriminating nature and, besides, Scrotton is not sufficiently intelligent to assess what we say, only to pass it on verbatim."

The preparation room door opened. Yoland stepped out, carrying a laser pointer.

"Today," he began, "we look at nuclear power." He switched the pointer on, moving the dot of red light over the diagram. "This is a plan of a nuclear power station. It looks complicated but is, in fact, quite simple in principle. A controlled nuclear reaction creates great heat that raises the temperature of water in a sealed system. This turns to steam, which drives massive turbines operating huge electrical generators. There are different types of nuclear power stations, but they all operate along basically the same lines. The fuel used in the reactor . . ." he moved the pinprick of light over the diagram once more ". . . is most often uranium-235."

"If it's in a sealed system, sir," Sebastian inquired, "how is the reaction controlled?"

"A good question, Gillette," Yoland responded. "To understand this, you need to know of what the reaction consists."

Yoland leaned his elbows on the demonstration bench. "Come nearer, everybody. Scrotton," he ordered as an aside, "the second diagram, please."

Scrotton obediently hung another diagram over the first. It depicted a uranium atom.

The club members edged forwards. Both Pip and Tim felt in their pockets for their clickers.

"The uranium atom," Yoland explained, "is what we call unstable. Under certain conditions, it attempts to divide in two. This is called fission. When it divides, particles of it are given off. Normally, when the uranium atom splits, the nucleus of it — the core of it — forms a barium nucleus, a krypton nucleus and three spare particles called neutrons." The laser spot hovered over a drawing of an atom splitting into two, with three small particles moving off to one side.

"These neutrons," Yoland continued, shifting the laser beam, "collide with other uranium atoms and cause them to vibrate. This creates heat. To control this, there are placed in the reactor what are known as control rods. These are frequently made of graphite, which absorbs some of the neutrons. Thus, by inserting or removing these rods you can manage the emission of heat. Additionally, the fuel — the uranium — can be immersed in a medium of carbon dioxide — a gas heavier than air — water or heavy water to further slow the particles down. This medium of gas or liquid also transfers the heat to make the steam."

"Heavy water?" a club member questioned.

"That," Yoland explained, "is water with its two ordinary hydrogen atoms replaced by two deuterium atoms. Deuterium is an isotope of hydrogen."

As he spoke, Pip observed the teacher. He looked hard into each pupil's face, his eyes intent, as if he was deliberately focusing on something, his lips vaguely smiling. Pip and Tim fingered their clickers, ready to defend themselves.

"Finally," Yoland announced just before the bell rang for the end of lunch break, "a fortnight today, on the first Friday back after vacation, we shall be going on a club outing. I have booked the school mini-bus and you are all excused from your afternoon classes." He handed an envelope to each pupil. "Give these to your parents and ask them to sign the permission slip."

"Where are we going?" one boy asked.

"I have arranged," Yoland said with all the panache of a circus ringmaster, "for us to have a guided tour of the Jasper Point nuclear power station."

This news was greeted with a babble of excitement by all the club members but three . . .

When Pip and Tim went down to breakfast on Monday morning, they noticed a large white and blue builders' van and a pick-up truck parked outside the coach house. Several men were unloading a cement mixer from the truck. Others were removing sacks of mortar, tools, bricks and lengths of drainpipe from the van.

"New drains," said Mrs. Ledger, "and that means you two are coming to Exington with me."

Pip and Tim looked in dismay at each other. This was not how they had intended starting off vacation.

"We'll be all right here, Mum," urged Pip. "We won't get in the way, or underfoot, or anything."

Their mother was adamant.

"Your father's got a storyboard to get through for a shoot next week, and he doesn't want to have any distractions. The builders will be enough," she added as, outside, one of the workmen started up the cement mixer, the engine puttering into noisy life.

"Promise," Pip pleaded.

"Twenty minutes, out by the car," Mrs. Ledger responded, unmoved.

By the time they reached the town, the High Street was already a bustling morning market, the pavements crowded with shoppers. Mrs. Ledger found it very difficult to find somewhere to park and was finally forced to drive to the top floor of the parking garage, a place she disliked intensely for, as she said several times as they ascended the ramps, driving in circles made her dizzy.

For the next hour, Pip and Tim traipsed behind their mother, following her from a pharmacy to a stationer's, a bookshop and, finally, a fabric shop where she spent at least twenty minutes rummaging through vast piles of curtain samples. It was late morning by the time they finally left the town for the supermarket on the outskirts.

"Can we sit in the car?" Pip asked. "I'm exhausted."

"Out of the question!" replied Mrs. Ledger with a finality both of her children knew only too well. "You're coming to the supermarket with me. Tim, get me a large cart."

The first area Mrs. Ledger visited was the fruit and vegetable section. At the far end were flower stands, by which an old lady stood inspecting bunches of tiger lilies and sprigs of waxy-petaled lilac-colored Thai orchids.

Her attention taken by the blossoms, the elderly woman did not notice a young man in a creased, mud-spattered leather jacket lingering nearby. He was in his mid-twenties, dressed in worn jeans, dirty sneakers and a sweatshirt. His jacket was zipped up the front, loose-fitting and probably several sizes too big for him, but the elasticated waist was tight around his belt.

"Scum alert!" Tim muttered to his sister.

When the old lady stretched for a bunch of flowers, the young man quickly reached for her shopping bag on the baby seat of her cart. In seconds, he had her purse and was about to slip it into his pocket when he spied Pip and Tim observing him. He immediately dropped the purse and kicked it under the woman's cart. Then, he touched her elbow to catch her attention and, bending down, picked up the purse, saying, " 'Scuse me, darlin', dropped yer purse, love?"

She thanked him profusely and he walked away with a crestfallen look.

"What a slimeball!" Pip muttered. "If we hadn't seen him . . ."

It took them several minutes to find their mother. Much to Pip and Tim's continual annoyance, she did not go around the supermarket according to the layout of the aisles but the make-up of her shopping list, which was categorized. Meat and fish, because they were main courses, were listed together despite the fact that the fish counter was at the opposite end of the store from the butchery department. When they caught up with her, she was by the bakery counter.

"Not much longer," she said encouragingly as they came up to her. "If you like, I'll meet you by the checkout."

As they sauntered off, the man in the leather jacket once again caught Tim's eye. He was in the beauty products and cosmetics aisle, facing a set of shelves loaded with men's toiletries. On the floor by his side was a supermarket basket containing some ordinary groceries. Just as Tim caught sight of him, he saw the man take down a bottle of expensive eau de Cologne, study the packaging for a moment and then, believing he was not being watched, hide it inside his jacket.

Tim hurried after Pip, who had walked on ahead of him.

"Hang on," he said, nodding slightly over his shoulder. "Slimer in action again at four o'clock high."

"You play too many war games," Pip chided him, but she gave a quick glance in the man's direction just in time to catch him tucking another item into his clothing.

When he picked up his basket, and moved on, Pip and Tim followed him at a distance. He paused here and there to openly put items in the basket, but he also surreptitiously filched a half-bottle of whiskey and a full bottle of Southern Comfort, putting them into his jacket and easing them around the side so that they did not bulge in the front. Finally, zipping the jacket up to his neck, he made for the checkout lines.

"Do you think they've a store detective or a security guard or something?" Pip asked. "We ought to tell someone."

"Naw to that!" said Tim dismissively. "This is a task for the punitors."

Pip looked into her brother's face. There was a mischievous glint in his eye.

"First test of PP," Tim continued.

"PP?" Pip queried.

"Punitor power!" Tim answered.

"Sebastian said the power would come when we needed it," Pip remarked. "Nothing happened when the boy pinched the purse."

"Maybe it all happened too quickly," Tim answered. "Maybe it takes a bit for the power to kick in."

The man joined the one-basket-only line. When it came to his turn, he put his basket on the shelf at the end of the conveyor belt and began to unload it. Pip and Tim positioned themselves in the adjacent line to watch.

"We can't just stand here," Pip said.

"See his jacket?" Tim said. "Concentrate on it."

"Concentrate? His jacket . . . !"

"Just do it, sis. Just do it!"

Tim half closed his eyes. He might have been praying.

When his basket was empty, the young man bent down to put it on the pile of others under the end of the counter. As he did so, Tim heard the jacket zipper start to unwind.

"Fun time," he muttered to Pip.

The man remained bent double. Tim could see he was fumbling with the zipper, trying to tug it up. It would not budge. He stopped and it slipped a little further down. By now, he was gripping it hard, sweat breaking out on his brow. Yet the zipper would not fasten and, as soon as he relaxed his grip, it edged lower towards his waist.

"Are you all right?" the woman manning the checkout inquired, while all around, people were starting to pay attention to the man's peculiar behavior.

By now, he was getting very anxious. The zipper was continuing its inexorable slide downward but, despite his increasingly frantic fumbling, he was unable to stop it. Finally, it reached the catch at the bottom, which suddenly snapped open. On to the floor fell a scattering of stolen items. The bottle of whiskey shattered, causing nearby shoppers to jump backward. Over the checkout, a strobe light started to flash as an alarm sounded in the ceiling. Two security guards appeared, running down the aisles. They apprehended the thief, marching him away towards the rear of the store.

"So that's what being a punitor's like!" Tim exclaimed with unsuppressed glee.

Mrs. Ledger knocked on Tim's bedroom door, carrying a tray of corned beef and pickle sandwiches, three glasses and a bottle of lemonade.

"Room service," she said cheerily.

"Thanks, Mum," Tim replied, quickly followed by Sebastian, who courteously said, "That's most considerate of you, Mrs. Ledger."

"Sandra, remember?" Mrs. Ledger retorted.

"Toady," Tim whispered, grinning.

Spread across the floor were Ordnance Survey maps, sheets of printer paper, pencils, scissors, a roll of tape, rulers, set squares, a pocket calculator, and a hiker's compass.

"What are you up to?" Mrs. Ledger inquired.

"Planning what we're going to do over vacation," Pip answered non-committally.

When her mother had gone, Pip aligned Sebastian's glass ruler with Rawne Barton, the hill fort, the Church of Saint Benedict and the Blessed Raymond Lull in Brampton, another church in a village two miles farther on and an ancient bridge over a river on a stretch of Roman road. Tim added another of his rulers with Sebastian adding a third and fourth. Finally, the line ended at a low headland on the coast not far from a small fishing village called Cockleton.

For a moment, Tim stared at the map and then said, "When was this published?"

Pip turned over a corner of the sheet, studied the bottom margin and replied, "Crown copyright, 1966."

Tim pointed to the headland. Clearly printed over the sea next to it were the words: Jasper Point.

"I think," he said, "we'll find they've done a bit of building there since then."

Getting up from the floor and taking care not to step on the map, Tim sat at his computer and logged on to the British Energy Web site.

" 'The Jasper Point nuclear power station,' " he read as the screen cleared and a picture of it unrolled, " 'is an advanced gas-cooled reactor which went online in 1976.

There are actually two reactors at Jasper Point producing 1,210 megawatts of electricity each at full capacity. This is sufficient to provide electricity to about a million homes.' Now that," Tim concluded, "is pretty major power."

"Pretty major power," Pip reiterated thoughtfully, "but what part does it play in Yoland's scheme?"

Twelve

Power to Behold

For the first few days of vacation week, Pip, Tim and Sebastian decided there was little they could do. Pip cycled past Yoland's bungalow a few times, but there were no signs of activity there other than a double-glazing worker putting the finishing touches to the new window. Twice, Tim took his mountain bike and risked riding at breakneck speed downhill through the wood in which Scrotton lived, yet all he saw were foraging squirrels and pheasants. As for Sebastian, he was absent throughout the daylight hours, only reappearing at dusk.

On the Wednesday evening, Sebastian summoned Pip and Tim to his underground chamber.

"I do not know exactly what Yoland's course of action will be," he stated. "I am not acquainted with the methodology of applying spell keys. However, I have drawn some conclusions. The first concerns the gold nobles. I do not think these are being employed in the making of the spell keys. I therefore deduce that they have another function. These coins are very valuable, both for their gold content and as historical artifacts.

Gold is the best substance with which to engender greed. I believe the coins feature in the spell as a mechanism for corrupting others or for distracting them from the evil he is undertaking."

"I've been thinking, too," Tim declared. "One of Yoland's aims is to spread evil. Right?"

"Indeed," Sebastian concurred.

"Now, what is evil?" Tim went on.

"Evil is wickedness," Sebastian explained, "a force the opposite of righteousness."

"Exactly," Tim said. "A force. And what is electricity if it isn't a force of some sort? And, to use archaic speak, therein I deduce lies the crux of our conundrum."

Pip scowled at Tim and remarked sharply, "You've got to be such a smart . . ." And then she fell silent.

"Penny dropped, sis?" Tim asked. "What does a nuclear power station do? It creates electricity and feeds it into the National Grid and, from there, to every building in Britain."

"In ancient times," Sebastian cut in, "power such as this traveled along ley lines . . ."

". . . but now," Tim continued, "it goes along copper wires to every wall socket in Britain. If Yoland has his way, every power point will become a portal for evil. Plug in your toaster and what have you got?"

"A gizmo radiating evil," said Pip in a voice muted by the horror of the thought.

"One thing I just don't get," Tim said. "What's the point of spreading evil about? How can Yoland benefit from it?"

"He benefits not from the evil itself," Sebastian explained, "but the anarchy this creates in the breakdown of law. Broadcast evil and you will not only create widespread wickedness but cause the disintegration of morality and, in turn, society. By the widespread stealing of souls, Yoland will control many thousands, perhaps many millions of people."

"So Yoland is out to rule the world!" Tim exclaimed. "Sounds like a case for the Caped Crusader!"

"Excuse me," Pip interrupted. "This isn't *Spider-Man Two*. It really is time you woke up and smelled the coffee, Tim."

"Spider-Man doesn't have a cape," Tim replied pedantically.

"Whoever," Pip retorted glibly.

"I am sure," Sebastian remarked, "Tim is already awake—" he sniffed the air "—and I sense no aroma of coffee."

Thursday morning dawned cold and clear, the sky a piercing blue, the sunlight stark but chill. The first of the winter's frosts shone on the grass, catching the sunlight like powdered glass.

Tim left the house at eight o'clock, wearing a dark-green padded fishing jacket, his feet encased in Wellington boots and long woolen socks lined with newspaper, a trick his grandfather had taught him. He could hear Grandpa Ledger's voice now: *There's good reason why those who have no home sleep under yesterday's headlines. The layers of paper trap the heat.* In his left hand, Tim carried an old army canvas gas-mask case and, in his right, a dark-blue fiberglass coarse fishing rod fitted with a rear-drag feeder reel, 300 meters of black four-pound-breaking-strain line and a lure made of rubber that looked like a newt. His fishing jacket was smeared with several seasons' worth of fish slime and blood that had resisted his mother's every effort to remove it.

Arriving at the river bank, Tim slowly made his way upstream, watching out for the telltale dash of silver in the pools that might indicate a school of fish being scattered by a pike. And he was after pike.

Downstream from the old bridge, the current had scoured out a deep, black pool next to the stone pier. If there was a pike worth catching in that stretch of the river it would, Tim reasoned, be there. Putting his bag down on the bank, he positioned himself upriver from the pool and cast downstream, pulling the artificial newt slowly up the current, at such a speed as would make its rubber tail waver from side to side as if it were alive and swimming.

On the fourth cast, Tim saw a jack pike of about three pounds swim up to it, inspect it, veer away and snatch a straggler from the rearguard of a shoal of minnows before swiftly heading across the river and under the roots of a willow overhanging the far bank.

The pike's appetite temporarily satisfied, Tim reeled the artificial newt in and, sitting down on the bank, removed it from the thin steel trace at the end of his line. Putting it in his lure box, he studied his other spinners and chose a silver-and-green spotted spoon in its place.

There was no point in immediately casting for the pike, and Tim was reluctant to try and tempt it out from the willow roots for risk of snaring his line, so he leaned back, his spine fitting between two courses of the stonework on the bridge pier. Even through his padded jacket, the masonry was sharp and cold.

Across the river, austere and dark behind the trees, the concave bowl of the quarry face loomed upward, the top fringed with bushes against the morning sky. As Tim looked at the rock face, he saw something moving up it. At first, he thought someone was rappeling. Several times in the summer, he had watched rock-climbers making their way up the wall of stone when he was fly-fishing. However, this figure seemed different. The rock-climbers tended to move smoothly, with a careful deliberation. This figure was jerky, its legs and arms out-stretched, the knees and elbows kept at right angles.

Curious, Tim put his fishing rod down in the grass and, finding a shallow stretch in the river, he waded over to the far bank and edged his way through the boulders and bushes. Gradually, he made his way closer to the quarry face.

Crouching behind a boulder, Tim cast his eye over the cliff before him. At first, he could make out nothing moving except a falcon strutting daintily along the edge of a fissure. Yet, no sooner had Tim seen it than it took to the wing, soaring into the air to ride an updraft, whisking away over the top of the quarry.

Close to where the bird had been perching, a figure appeared. Dressed in dark-brown clothing and seem-ing to hug the rock face with every curve of its body, it rapidly moved sideways across the sheer wall. Its jerking movement reminded Tim of a bat.

It was a moment before Tim realized what he was watching.

It was Scrotton.

Then, to Tim's horror, another Scrotton appeared from the debris of loose stones at the foot of the quarry face, crabbing up to join the first. A third Scrotton materialized and ascended the sheer surface, following in exactly the same footholds and handholds as the other two.

Tim retreated to the river as quickly as his Wellington boots would allow, keeping as low as possible, but to no avail. He was still twenty meters from the water's edge when he heard a thrashing of the undergrowth behind him. Glancing around, he saw the three Scrottons loping through the bushes, the branches lashing their faces. They made no attempt to brush them aside. When they came up to a bramble patch, the thorns snagged their hair and skin, but they paid them not the slightest heed.

"Hell's bells!" Tim whispered.

He kicked off his boots and hurled them at the leading Scrotton. It batted them aside with a bunched fist, hardly breaking its stride. Barefoot and regardless of sharp stones or thorny twigs, Tim accelerated to a sprint, his feet kicking up plumes of dusty earth on the path. He was grateful for the newspaper-lined socks.

At the river bank, he launched himself into the water, stumbling over the rocks just under the surface. The Scrottons slid to a halt, apparently reluctant to enter the water.

Reaching down by his feet, Tim picked up a smooth, round stone the size of an apple and hurled it at his pursuers, now less than five meters away. The first Scrotton ducked. The second took a glancing blow on its brow and started to growl loudly through bared teeth. It glanced from one to the other of its companions then began to gradually advance into the river, feeling carefully for loose stones underfoot. Tim edged backward. The water was icy. Already, he could barely feel his toes.

"Told you not to mess wiv me, didn' I?" the first Scrotton muttered. His teeth were yellow, like an old dog's, and chipped.

"Don't learn too good, do ya?" asked the second. Its words were slurred as if it had a speech defect.

The third Scrotton hopped forward, its feet splashing. Tim jumped backward, almost losing his balance, flailing his arms to keep upright.

"'Bout this time tomorrer," the third Scrotton prophesied, "they'll find yer sorry little carcass a long way downstream, caught under an over'angin' willer."

"Much cryin' 'n' wailin' and gnashin' of teeth in Rawne Barton tomorrer night," predicted the second Scrotton.

"Diggin' of 'oles and sayin' of prayers," added the third.

Tim looked hastily around for a weapon. Riding directly towards him on the current was a stout tree branch.

"Forget 'bout that!" the first Scrotton exclaimed. He reached under the water, picking up a large stone and tucking it into his neck shot-put style. "Told ya I was good at gym," he chortled, his throat rattling as if it was full of phlegm.

Spinning around, Scrotton hurled the stone, striking the branch in the center, cracking it in two. The splash knocked it out of the current. Tim impotently watched his weapon drift away.

Hunching themselves down, the Scrottons started to advance in a line, their arms hanging at their sides, their hands in the water, feeling for rocks as they moved nearer.

Looking behind himself, Tim wondered if he could get to his fishing gear before the Scrottons reached him. If he could, the rod might serve as a weapon and, if they came to fighting at close quarters, the lead-filled priest in his bag might serve as a handy sap.

Then, suddenly, it dawned on him. Fumbling at the buttons of the breast pocket of his fishing shirt, Tim thrust his hand inside, feeling for the rowan disc. Finding it, he held it out and started to revolve it.

"Gha! Gha!" Scrotton grunted. It was a rasping sound halfway between a laugh and a snort. "Look!" He turned to address his supporters. "'E's got a rowan circle! Fat lotta good that'll do 'im, eh!"

Bending down, Scrotton found a small stone and hurled it at Tim. It struck his hand. His fingers opened involuntarily and the rowan disc fell into the river, spinning in an eddy on the edge of the main current. Tim, ignoring the advancing Scrottons, threw himself after it, stumbling over boulders in the river bed. The waves he made drove it further away. Scrotton also made to grab the disc, but Tim beat him to it. He quickly revolved it in his fingers.

The Scrottons stopped in their tracks, looking from one to the other in a perplexed fashion. Scrotton himself stood firm, his eyes closed. He was, Tim knew, fighting the power of the rowan disc.

Gradually, Tim stepped backward. Scrotton made no

attempt to follow him. The power of the rowan disc was holding him. Tim did not take his eyes off Scrotton.

Suddenly, there was a frantic splashing in the river. The Scrottons were scrambling on to the bank and vanishing between the boulders. Scrotton himself turned and followed them.

Through the quarry rode four women exercising their horses. One waved and called out, "Catch anything?"

Tim returned the wave, putting the rowan disc back in his pocket, buttoning it up once more.

"Not yet," he shouted back.

Arriving at a thick clump of hazel saplings, the riders followed the path behind it. Tim could make out their shapes through the branches but, by the time they reached the other side of the thicket, their outlines had faded and disappeared. The sound of the horses' hooves died out instantly.

"If that's not being saved by the cavalry," Tim said aloud to himself, "I don't know what is . . ."

Deciding to abandon his Wellington boots, Tim climbed the bank and, gathering up his fishing gear, set off for home. Glancing back at the quarry, he could just make out a Scrotton setting off up the rock face, leaving a trail of water as it rose higher.

Pip was in the sitting room when Tim arrived back at Rawne Barton. Making a detour past his father's study to borrow his binoculars, Tim poked his head around the door and said perfunctorily, "Word, sis. Now! And call up the maestro!"

Leading the other two up to the attic, and kneeling

by the old window set in the gable end of the house, Tim spat on the glass to loosen the grime and polished it with his handkerchief.

"Look at this!" he ordered, adjusting the focus on the binoculars and passing them to Sebastian. "Over at the quarry. What do you see?"

Sebastian saw nothing until Tim showed him how to refine the focus. Then he briefly studied the quarry and handed the binoculars to Pip.

"Scrotton!" she exclaimed.

"Look again, sis."

"Plural!" retorted Pip. "I can see two of them."

"There's at least three," Tim replied. "I came face to face with them at the river. Saved in the nick of time by the rowan disc and . . ."

"Gentlefolk on horseback?" Sebastian asked.

"How did you know . . . ?" Tim began.

"Do not think, because I am not with you, that I am not with you," Sebastian replied enigmatically.

"What are the Scrottons up to?" Pip wondered, lowering the binoculars.

"Shinning up and down," Tim said.

"Yes, but why?"

"Think," Sebastian said, "of a butterfly newly emerged from its chrysalis. It does not appear immediately to fly away. It lingers for a while, moving its wings, waiting for the veins therein to fill with blood, expand the tissue in the framework. It flexes its legs, unfurls its antennae, unrolls its proboscis, raises and lowers its abdomen . . ."

"Do you mean to say," Pip asked incredulously, "that these Scrottons are — *newly hatched*?"

"You may put it in such words," Sebastian replied.

"Then where are they coming from?" Tim mused.

"Later, when it is safe, I shall show you," Sebastian answered.

At four o'clock that afternoon, when the sun was already beginning to drop, they left the house, crossed Rawne Ground, waded the river and made their way into the quarry. Tim wore a pair of old sneakers.

Nearing the loose stones that had fallen from the quarry face over the years, Sebastian paused and, telling the others to wait several paces behind him, he started scrambling up the gentle slope, arriving at the point where it reached the base of the sheer rock face. Here, he began to excavate the scree, pushing stones behind him. For several minutes, he bent forward and dug with his hands. Eventually, he stood up.

"Come here," he invited Pip and Tim.

They joined Sebastian. In the loose shale and stones, there was what at first looked like a crumbled transparent plastic sack, the size of a small trash bag.

"What is it?" Tim inquired.

"To continue my allusion to an emerging butterfly," Sebastian said, "this is, as it were, the shell of a chrysalis from which a replicate Scrotton has emerged."

"You have to be joking!" Tim exploded.

Sebastian made no reply but the look on his face spoke volumes.

Thirteen

Winds of Wickedness

At the head of the line waiting to enter the biology laboratory on the first day back after vacation was Scrotton. Although his clothing was as creased and disheveled as usual, it was much cleaner. He made no effort to communicate with anyone else in the line and stood staring at his feet.

"Think that's the original Scrotton we've grown to know and love?" Tim whispered to Pip.

Sebastian, overhearing him, shook his head and said, "That is one of the replicates. His clothing is clean because he has just hatched."

"Like a butterfly," Pip murmured. "The colors are brightest when it has only just left its chrysalis."

The laboratory door was opened by a short-haired, handsome young man in his early twenties wearing a blue blazer, khaki trousers, a white shirt and a tie with a university crest embroidered upon it. His suede shoes were well brushed.

"Come in," he invited the class, "and sit in your usual places, please."

The pupils filed in and fanned out between the benches.

"My name," the teacher began, "is Mr. David Loudacre and I'm the substitute teacher taking Miss Bates's classes this week."

"That's a weird name," one of the cheekier boys remarked, trying it on with a new teacher who was, judging by his age and appearance, fresh out of college.

Mr. Loudacre made no immediate response, but his face hardened to stone and he stared intensely at the boy through eyes narrowed to little more than malevolent slits.

"And your name is . . . ?" he inquired at length, each word redolent with anger.

"Newbould, sir," the boy murmured and he shrank down in his seat, pretending to busy himself with the contents of his bag.

"Let's get this quite clear from the start," Mr. Loudacre began, surveying the class. "I will abide no rudeness, no insolence and no tomfoolery. Now," he picked up a pile of printed worksheets, "Miss Bates has set a project for you to do which I shall supervise. It concerns the skeleton of a bird." He turned and opened the door of a cupboard. Inside were a number of animal skeletons mounted on wire frames. "You," he pointed to Scrotton. "I wonder if you'd mind doing the honors and take out the skeleton of the chicken."

Without replying, Scrotton went to the cupboard and gingerly removed the specimen, sliding its base carefully onto the teacher's bench.

"Thank you," Mr. Loudacre said, revolving the skeleton

so that it was side-on to the class. Then, addressing Scrotton again, he added, "Hand out these sheets."

Scrotton took a wedge of printed drawings of the chicken's skeleton and started to make his way around the class.

"As I indicate the bones of the skeleton," Mr. Loudacre continued, "I want you to label your diagrams."

There was a general fumbling for pencils and rulers.

"You will notice," the teacher continued, "that a bird's bones are particularly thin. This is to reduce weight and permit a degree of flexibility in order to make flight possible. If birds were built like Bruce Willis they'd never leave the ground."

He laughed self-indulgently at his own joke, removed a ballpoint pen from his pocket and began to indicate different bones, writing the names of some of them on the whiteboard with a green marker. For thirty minutes, the class concentrated on labeling the bones. When they were done, Mr. Loudacre began dictating notes as to the function of each major bone, pointing out that the larger they were the more muscle attachment they carried. At the end of the lesson, the labeled diagrams were collected, once again by Scrotton, and the class was dismissed. Mr. Loudacre stood by the door to see them out of the room and down the corridor.

"So what do you think?" Tim asked as they walked out into the playground.

"He chose Scrotton," Sebastian replied.

"And he asked him to do the honors," Tim added. "Who does that remind you of? And did you see how he looked at Newbould? If looks could kill . . ." He drew his index finger across his throat.

"Furthermore," Sebastian continued, "he's a biologist — the study of life."

"Lastly," Tim concluded, "there's his name."

"What're you two going on about?" Pip inquired, taking a muesli bar out of her pocket and unwrapping it.

"Nothing strike you as odd, sis?" Tim asked.

Pip looked perplexed.

"About what?"

"Miss Bates's stand-in. The substitute guy."

"No. Why should it? Substitute teachers're as common as wasps at picnics. Here today, gone next week."

"Think about it, sis."

Pip shrugged and put the bar between her teeth.

"Think of his name," Tim pressed her. "Mr. Loudacre. Mr. David Loudacre, Mr. D. Loudacre."

It was as if Pip had forgotten she had the muesli bar in her mouth. She froze, and it was at least fifteen seconds before her hand lowered and she removed the bar from between her lips.

"Oh! My God!" she whispered timorously. "It's de Loudéac. It's Malodor!"

"Couldn't you tell from the pendant?" Tim said.

Pip looked a little awkward and said, "I've not got it on."

"What!" Tim replied, his anger roused. "Why the hell not? What do you think it's for?"

"I didn't want Scrotton to try and nick it again. It was Queen Joan's," she added defensively.

"I don't care if it was Cleopatra's or the Queen of Sheba's. You . . ."

"This disputatious quarrel is academic," Sebastian interjected. "What is done is done."

211

"He must have recognized us," said Tim.

"Probably," Sebastian answered. "Yet it matters not, for he will not have expected you to have recognized him, and therefore he will not feel threatened or at risk. As for me," Sebastian looked himself up and down and ran his fingers through his hair. It had grown at least a centimeter since Pip had restyled it and had become distinctly spiky. "I hardly appear as I did."

"Say no more!" Tim exclaimed.

"I was not intending so to do," Sebastian replied.

"Shall we return to planet earth?" Pip suggested, regaining some of her composure. "What we want to know is why is he here and what's he up to?"

They reached the far corner of the playground and turned towards the horse chestnut tree. Most of the leaves had fallen, so it was easy to be sure that Scrotton was not squatting in the boughs like a malicious rook.

"It seems abundantly apparent," Sebastian said, "that Loudacre, de Loudéac, Malodor — call him what you will — is assisting Yoland in the creation of the Scrotton replicates. As to what other part he will play in the spreading of evil, time will reveal."

Just before they left school that afternoon, the Atom Club members gathered in Chemistry Laboratory One, to be addressed by Yoland.

"On Friday, as I am sure I need not remind you," he announced, "we are making our visit to Jasper Point, departing in the school minibus at noon. You will bring packed lunches, which are to be consumed en route. School bags may be taken, but they must be left in the minibus during our visit. No valuables may be brought.

Do not bring a camera. Photography is not permitted at Jasper Point for obvious security reasons. You will be required to bring a ballpoint pen."

The laboratory door opened.

"As you will all know from your primary school, all school outings must be accompanied by two or more members of staff . . ."

The club members looked around. Tim, Pip and Sebastian had no need to: they knew who had just entered.

Loudacre approached the demonstration desk and stood next to Yoland.

"With the German exchange, we are somewhat short of teachers this week," Yoland said, "so Mr. Loudacre has kindly agreed to step into the breach."

Yoland smiled at Loudacre and turned back to the pupils.

"I need not say that your behavior must be exemplary," he went on. "Not only are you ambassadors for the school but you are also entering an environment fraught with danger. You will do exactly as you are told at all times. You do not wander off, you pay attention to the Jasper Point staff, who will not only be mindful of your safety, but will impart to you much fascinating information of which you will take notes on worksheets provided. We should be on site for about two hours and return to the school at approximately four o'clock. Kindly remind your parents. School buses will not depart until after our return. Any questions? Very well, off you go. I'm sure we'll all have a most interesting day."

As they left the laboratory, Tim muttered under his breath, "Of that we can be as sure as big tigers have large stripes."

Fourteen

Half-lives, Half-deaths

The white minibus was parked to one side of the school gates, the school crest and name emblazoned on the side. Yoland sat in the driver's seat, against which leaned the old attaché case Pip had last seen under the desk in his study. At the bus door stood Loudacre, marking off each pupil's name on a list as they boarded. To each he smiled pleasantly and made a friendly comment.

Passing close to him, Pip just discerned the faint odor of a carton of apple juice past its sell-by date and sour milk. It made her feel slightly sick, although whether from the odor of the teacher or her own fear she was not sure. The thought of traveling in the confines of a minibus with Malodor was not an enticing one.

"Got Queen's Joan's bauble on?" Tim asked Pip in an undertone.

"No point, really," she answered. "We all know where the evil is. It would be vibrating all day long like a bee in your bra."

"A vespa in your vest," Sebastian suggested.

"A what?" Tim retorted. "A motor scooter in her vest!"

"*Vespa*," Sebastian added disconsolately, his attempt at a joke falling flat, "is Latin for a wasp."

Once in the vehicle, Pip, Sebastian and Tim sat about halfway back. Loudacre installed himself in the seat by the door, while Scrotton was by the emergency exit at the back. On the penultimate row of seats was a large, dark-blue bag with handles and printed with the name of a leading sports-equipment manufacturer.

"Please, sir," Tim asked Loudacre with feigned naivete, "what's that bag for?"

Loudacre looked at it as if noticing it for the first time and replied, "I've no idea. I think it must have been left by the last people to use the bus. That, I think, was the First Eleven soccer team yesterday afternoon."

"Like, yeah!" Tim muttered to Sebastian. "Sergeant Major Form-a-Line forgetting the gear? I think not . . ."

Yoland started the engine, and a cloud of smoke erupted briefly from the exhaust.

"Does everyone have their seat belt on?" Yoland called out.

Loudacre made his way down the minibus like an air hostess checking passengers before takeoff and confirmed they did. The gearbox grated and the minibus lurched forward.

Taking a main road towards the coast, it was not long before there appeared on the horizon five huge square buildings, painted gray, from which rows of tall, high-tension pylons ranged out across the countryside.

"Looks like they're marching across the land, a steel army on the advance," said Pip.

As she spoke, she caught sight of Loudacre's face. A tiny smile flickered across his lips.

Yoland slowed the minibus, turning left off the main road down a well-maintained side road. On the corner was a small signpost to Cockleton and a much larger one which read: *National Power — Jasper Point Nuclear Power Station: 6 miles.*

"Six miles!" Pip exclaimed. "Those buildings must be vast. I thought they were no more than a mile off."

Some way down the road, they arrived at the village of Cockleton. On entering it, Yoland had to pull onto the side of the road to allow a convoy of seven massive, high-sided trucks, preceded by a police escort, to pass in the opposite direction.

"Nuclear waste," Tim remarked.

Most of the cottages, some of them thatched, faced on to the road. They were splattered with mud as high as the windows. The bushes in the gardens were discolored with a thick layer of dingy dust. The pub sign badly needed repainting, and the thatch was tattered where the trucks had rubbed against the eaves.

"Must've been a pretty place before they built the power station," Tim remarked, as the minibus drove along what must once have been a picturesque dockside. It was now just a derelict quay with the hulk of a fishing boat lying half sunk in mud, surrounded by rank reeds.

As they left the village, Loudacre leaned across from his seat and started to talk to Yoland. Sebastian casually touched Tim's shoulder and cast a glance at the sports bag. Tim gave it a cursory look, then touched his foot against Pip's ankle under the seat. She followed his eye.

Whatever was in the bag seemed to be moving.

Scrotton, catching Tim's eye, snarled, "Wot yer think yer starin' at?" He gave the bag a short, vicious kick.

The power station security gates were manned by two security guards and four policemen each wearing a black flak jacket and armed with — as Tim noted with a shiver of excitement — an MP5 sub-machine gun.

"Best anti-terrorist weapon in the world," Tim declared, with all the eagerness of a gun fanatic at an international arms fair.

After the security guards had inspected Yoland's pass, the gates opened electronically and the minibus moved forward to park in a visitor's space. No sooner had Loudacre opened the doors than a man in white overalls and a gaudy-yellow hard hat approached them.

"Good afternoon," he greeted them cheerily. "Welcome to Jasper Point. If you would all gather around me? Teachers as well."

Everybody tumbled out of the bus and encircled him.

"My name is Mr. Clayton, and I am your official guide this afternoon," he introduced himself. "Our tour will take about an hour and a half. Before we set off, perhaps you would all like to pin one of these on your clothing." From his pocket, he produced a number of orange plastic badges. "These," he explained, "are called dosimeters. They display how much radiation you have been exposed to. By the end of the afternoon, we shall see you have received no measurable radiation exposure at all. Contrary to public opinion, Jasper Point is very safe indeed. If you'll follow me?"

As they set off, the guide noticed that Yoland was carrying the attaché case.

"Excuse me, sir," he said, "but I'm afraid I must ask you to leave your case at reception."

"It only contains worksheets," Yoland explained and he unbuckled the flap, opening the case for inspection.

The guide took a brief look in it and said, "I'm afraid you must still leave it at reception, sir. Rules, I'm afraid. We live in uncertain times."

"Yeah, right!" Tim whispered to himself.

Yoland took out a batch of sheets held by a paper clip and, turning to Scrotton, said, "Do the honors, Scrotton."

As he handed them to Scrotton, Sebastian noticed Yoland slip a small padded envelope out of the attaché case and into his pocket. This done, he passed the case to the receptionist.

"He has the spell keys," he mouthed to Pip and Tim. They gave small nods of understanding.

Scrotton passed around the worksheets, and the party entered the first building. Everyone signed a computer screen with a stylus and was issued with a visitor's badge and a blue hard hat.

"I feel sorry for the next visitor who gets greaseball's hat," Pip said.

The formalities completed, they were led down a long corridor along the ceiling of which ran color-coded pipes and cables. As they went, their guide introduced them to the power station.

"Jasper Point," he announced, "is an AGR — an Advanced Gas-cooled Reactor — power station. In fact, we have two reactors here, A and B. The latter is currently shut down for maintenance, so we shall visit reactor-A. Each reactor produces enough electricity to ignite over ten million light bulbs. Now," he went on, opening another door onto a long passageway, "follow me."

"What gas is used in the reactor?" Tim asked.

"Carbon dioxide," came the reply. "It is heavier than air and comparatively inert. This means it cannot ignite or explode."

"Sir," Sebastian asked, "how hot is the gas in the reactor?"

"Approximately 460° Celsius," Mr. Clayton replied, "over four and a half times the boiling point of water."

"And I suppose it is under great pressure," Sebastian went on.

"Indeed, it is," Mr. Clayton confirmed. He ran a security card through a swipe reader on the wall and, opening an airlock door, declared, "This is the nerve center of Jasper Point."

Tim and Pip knew what line Sebastian's thoughts were taking. What had held back alchemical progress had been the inability to create extremely high temperatures and pressures. Now, here were both in one building — and so, too, were two corrupt alchemists of evil intent.

The pupils shuffled through the airlock to find themselves on a plate-glass-lined balcony. Below them, three men sat at a wide console of computer monitors, CCTV screens, meters and switches.

"This is the central control room," Mr. Clayton said.

"Almost all the processes are fully automated and operated from here. Let us move on to the reactor itself."

They made their way down a short passageway. Through the windows could be seen a maze of criss-crossing pipes and ducts running up the side of the adjacent building. Some leaked wisps of steam at their joints. The guide led them up a long flight of metal stairs into a vast hangar of a building.

"This is the reactor hall of the reactor-A building," Mr. Clayton said with evident pride.

They followed him into it. The interior was floodlit by powerful halogen arc lamps suspended from the roof at least fifty meters above.

"Where is the reactor?" asked someone.

"A good question," Mr. Clayton said. "In actual fact, the reactor is now directly beneath your feet. You are standing on it."

Everyone looked down at their shoes in wonderment.

The floor consisted of a patchwork of square metal plates, not unlike smooth manhole covers, highly polished and about a meter across.

"The reactor is over ten meters high and weighs more than 2,000 tons," the guide went on. "It is encased in a reinforced concrete shell over four meters thick."

"Is it working now?" one pupil inquired.

"It certainly is," Mr. Clayton answered. "At this minute, it is generating over 800 megawatts of electricity."

Yoland and Loudacre stood at the rear of the group of pupils, Scrotton close by. Tim watched them, but they seemed intent on the guide's lecture, so he transferred his attention back to Mr. Clayton. When he next looked back at the teachers, Scrotton was not there.

He nudged Pip and Sebastian.

"Can you see Scrotton anywhere?"

They glanced around and shrugged.

"Then where's he gone?"

"Nuclear fuel," the guide continued, "comes in the form of long rods or bars. New rods are lowered into — and spent ones removed from — the reactor by this mechanism here."

He pointed to a tall yellow-painted tower of skeletal metal girders. One entire side had platforms at regular intervals, with ladders leading up to them. The whole structure vaguely reminded Tim of an Olympic-sized-swimming-pool diving board. It extended almost to the roof high above.

"Beneath each of the plates under your feet is a fuel rod and a control rod," the guide went on, turning his back to the tower. "Once they are spent, they are removed . . ."

Out of the corner of her eye, Pip caught a movement behind the tower. Loudacre had detached himself from the tour group and was cautiously opening a steel emergency exit door at the back of the hall, looking over his shoulder as he did so.

Jutting her chin in his direction, she murmured, "It's beginning."

As soon as the door was more than ajar, Scrotton squeezed in, dragging the bag that had been on the minibus. Loudacre closed the door behind him. Once inside, Scrotton quickly unzipped the bag, and Loudacre removed several corked test tubes, the contents of which he scattered into the bag. Instantly, the fabric sides twitched violently and two dozen small Scrottons, not much larger than infants, emerged as if projected by a spring.

"Now we know . . . !" Tim exclaimed.

"De Loudéac's been busy," Sebastian observed.

As they watched, the Scrottons grew bigger. Within a few seconds they were the size of the original but, unlike him, stark naked. Their hairy bodies resembled those of unkempt monkeys afflicted by mange.

At that moment Mr. Clayton, who had been talking to Yoland and the party of pupils, caught sight of the new additions to his tour group.

"What the hell is going on?" he demanded, reaching for a walkie-talkie attached to his belt.

The pupils spun around. Standing in a line across the reactor floor were the Scrottons, Scrotton himself to the fore. For a moment there was silence, not a sound to be heard but the general background hum of the power station. Then one girl screamed. In an instant, the other girls joined in. The boys stood helpless, leaderless, unsure what to do, looking hopefully to the teachers for advice, but to no avail.

The words had hardly left Mr. Clayton's mouth when Yoland dropped something on the steel plates of the floor in front of him. It chimed dully and shimmered in the brilliant glare of the halogen arc lights. Forgetting his two-way radio, the guide bent down, picking it up in both hands and holding it close to his face, much as a curious child might examine something it had just found.

"It's one of the nobles," Tim said.

"As I suspected," Sebastian declared, "their use is to divert, to ensnare the wills of those who would prevent Yoland's plan. Gold fascinates all men. In its way, it too can steal their souls, as indeed you discovered when you could not let it go."

The Scrottons, now all a uniform size and indistinguishable from one another in their hairy nakedness, swung from platform to platform on the refueling tower, rising higher and higher. Others climbed pipes set against the wall. Some scampered over the floor on all fours, chasing each other in a madcap game of tag. Those on the tower leaped from it to the walls, screeching. The CCTV screens in the reactor hall showed their cavortings.

"What're they up to?" Pip pondered.

"Diverting attention," Sebastian replied.

"From what?" Tim considered.

At that moment, Pip said, "Where's Loudacre?"

They looked around. He was nowhere in sight.

"Heading for the control room, I would wager," Sebastian predicted. "Pip! Go after him. Tim and I will deal with the Scrottons and Yoland."

"Time to rumble!" Tim proclaimed.

Scrotton uttered a deep coughing bark, like a baboon's. The replicate Scrottons swung down from the refueling tower and walls. A dozen formed a circle around Yoland, facing out. They bared their teeth and grimaced like rabid dogs. Scrotton stood at the teacher's side. The other Scrottons began to herd the Atom Club members into a corner, prodding them and snarling. The girls clung to each other. Some were crying, others joined several of the boys in lashing out at the replicates, driving them back.

Turning to a boy called Den, Pip commanded, "Get everybody out. As fast as you can. Right out of the building. Ignore Scrotton."

"Which one?" replied the perplexed Den.

"All of them," Pip snapped back. "Especially the one with clothes on. And don't listen to a word the teachers say."

"But . . ." Den began.

"But nothing!" Pip screamed. "Don't ask dumb questions. Just do it."

Den was still hesitant, puzzled, unsure.

"What if . . . ?" he started.

"Forget what if!" Tim bellowed.

"Go out the way we came in," Pip demanded. "If you meet anyone, raise the . . ."

The remainder of her sentence was drowned by the ear-splitting clanging of alarm bells. Strobe lights began to flash high up on the walls.

"Where do we . . . ?" Den started to ask.

"Just get them out!" Pip hollered, her patience completely spent.

With that, she ran to the door they had entered by and swung it back. Halfway down the long flight of steps, she could make out Loudacre descending them. Without thinking, she set off after him, the Atom Club members, led by Den, stumbling after her.

In the center of the reactor floor, Yoland stood with his arms raised. Scrotton removed a long, polished steel tool from a rack on the wall. One end of it had a spanner-like terminal.

"Holy Kamoly!" Tim exclaimed to Sebastian. "That's got to be a tool for . . ."

There was no need for him to complete the sentence. Scrotton attached the spanner end of the bar to lugs in a floor panel and, with a twist and a heave, hauled it aside. There was an instant roar of escaping gas from inside the reactor. The floor panel flew across the hall to smash into the wall. On its flight, it struck one of the naked Scrottons, slicing open its chest to the ribs. The creature's scream was so high-pitched it was barely audible over the rush of escaping gas.

Alarm sirens screeched. The needles of gauges on the wall of the reactor hall began to quiver and spin. Colored diodes winked frantically on a switch- and light-board. Digital readouts rolled over so quickly their numbers were little more than a blur of red.

The force of the escaping gas clouded the air, forcing Scrotton to stagger backward. He put his hands to his face. Tim could see that the skin had been burned off his brow. It hung in tatters that he tore away with his hands.

Five power station engineers in orange protective clothing ran in, heading for Yoland, who had also been driven back by the blast of scalding gas. He threw a handful of nobles at them. They stopped in their tracks but, unable to pick the coins up with their heavy protective gloves, merely stood where they were, bending over, staring at them as if obsessed. Some Scrottons picked the nobles up and steered the engineers into a corner with Mr. Clayton, standing guard over them with an occasional growl or snarl.

An automated voice started repeating: *Radiation alert — radiation alert. All non-essential staff evacuate the reactor hall.*

"We've got to get out of here," Tim yelled to Sebastian over the din of the alarm and escaping gas. "Carbon dioxide's heavier than air. It'll fill this place in minutes — and it's radioactive."

Yoland removed the envelope from his pocket and tore it open. Chanting in a squealing voice, he took out four spell keys and, one by one, tossed them into the reactor. The force of the escaping gas took hold of them, and they rose high overhead before dropping to the floor, where they sparked in a tiny explosion and vanished.

He tried again. One disappeared into the reactor. The rest soared away and exploded either on the floor or against the walls.

"Scrotton," Yoland shouted, "tell Loudacre to reduce the reactor pressure, then come back here."

"If he succeeds in dropping the pressure," Tim said urgently, "the reactor will quickly overheat and melt down. Jasper Point'll become Chernobyl-by-the-Sea in less than thirty minutes."

Scrotton ran to the reactor hall door and disappeared.

The control room door was open when Pip reached it. Inside, the three controllers were hunched together on the floor, turning over gold nobles in their fingers.

Loudacre was standing at the semicircular reactor control console, moving slider switches to new settings. As Pip entered, he looked up.

Pip felt her face pale. Her knees grew weak and her hands shook. Sweat started to run down the back of her neck and trickle down her spine.

Fixing her eyes on the sliders, she thought briefly of the supermarket thief's zipper and concentrated hard. The numbers on a monitor above the desk began to gradually count down.

"So," Loudacre said, "that accursed alchemist's brat has made you a punitor."

Pip made no answer but concentrated harder on the sliders. The numbers continued to decline.

"You, a mere child, are no match for me," Loudacre declared dismissively.

Loudacre stepped back from the console. The sliders moved of their own volition. Pip tried to stop them but could not. The monitor continued to count down.

Thrusting her hand in her pocket, Pip removed her rowan disc. If she could not stop the controls with punitor powers, she reasoned, she could at least stop Loudacre — de Loudéac, Malodor.

"My will and skills," Loudacre continued, "developed over the centuries, against yours learned what — a week ago . . . ?"

Pip, keeping her hand by her side, revolved the disc. Loudacre saw the movement and looked at the disc in her hand. Pip spun it as quickly as she could, again and again.

"A brave try," Loudacre complimented her, "but I am immune to such fairground toys. They may work with Yoland. Yet he is hardly of my caliber. A novice by comparison."

The counter continued to fall, more quickly now, more steadily.

Pip kept turning the disc. It had to work.

Even at a distance of several meters, Pip could smell Loudacre's breath. It stank of putrefying meat, dead fish and rotting vegetation.

"A futile try," Loudacre muttered.

Pip surrendered and put the disc back in her pocket.

"You think I know you not?" he went on. "I have not forgotten . . ."

"And I have not forgotten you," Pip interrupted defiantly.

Loudacre's eyes narrowed. Through the slits of his eyelids they appeared to hold a fire deep within them, just as Yoland's did.

"I am sure that is so," he replied. "Nor shall you."

He pointed his left hand at Pip. She felt a strange sensation surge though her body, as if her flesh were shrinking around her skeleton.

"I can squeeze the life from you without even touching you," Loudacre threatened in not much more than a whisper. "Consider. You would be advised to be afeared of me. Terribly afeared."

Pip gasped for breath.

"Soon, you meddling runt, you will find air more precious than gold."

Loudacre turned his back on Pip, paying attention to the power station controls. The digital counter was still dropping.

Wheezing hard and feeling light-headed from lack

of oxygen, Pip glanced around. She had to do something. Mounted on the wall was a small green fire extinguisher under a notice that stated: *For Electrical Fires Only*. It was, Pip was certain, heavy enough to be of use as a weapon, if she had the strength to lift it. Yet, she considered, it might still serve her purpose.

She wrenched it from its mounting, hugged it to her chest with one arm and pulled the safety pin.

"Afeared of you!" she panted boldly. "Never!"

Loudacre turned around. Pip squeezed the extinguisher trigger. A long blast of argon and nitrogen gas hit him full in the face. He raised his hands in defense. The freezing gases, under pressure, peeled his skin away from his hands. Eventually, he fell against the console and slumped to the floor, whimpering and catching his breath.

When the extinguisher was empty, Pip lurched to the control room door. Once outside, her breathing became normal, and she headed as fast as she could up the stairs to the reactor hall.

Halfway up, she came face to face with Scrotton running pell-mell down towards her. Just a meter or two from her, he launched himself into midair, sailed over her head, landed by the control room door and disappeared inside.

Pip reached the reactor hall. Bursting into it, she saw Yoland standing close to the hole in the floor. The carbon-dioxide coolant was no longer rushing out under pressure. Alarm bells continued to ring. The Scrottons stood in a circle around him, facing out. Tim and Sebastian stood a few meters from the circle.

"What's happened?" she asked Tim.

"Pressure's down. Yoland's about to do the stuff. Where's Loudacre?"

"Out of the game," Pip answered. "The rowan disc and punitor power didn't work, so I put out his fire instead."

Yoland raised his arms as if in supplication. Out of his jacket pocket protruded the end of the envelope containing the spell keys.

"What is that?" Pip said.

From the opening in the reactor floor appeared a vague, miasmic face like those, Pip thought, one saw sometimes in clouds on summer days, only not as dense.

"The enemy," Sebastian replied succinctly.

"Whose enemy . . . ?"

She looked again. The face was friendly, smiling, happy. Then, in an instant, it was leering, its lip curled, its cheekbones prominent, its hair matted and long.

"Everyone's enemy," Tim said, taking his sister's hand.

"Everyone who is good of soul and deed, that is," Sebastian added.

"You mean . . ." Pip started.

"That," Sebastian confirmed, "is the satanic visage of Beelzebub, Lucifer, Mephisto, Ahriman . . ."

The automated voice changed. *Reactor malfunction — Reactor malfunction. Containment staff red alert. Containment staff red alert.*

The ethereal face turned as blue as an electric spark and opened its mouth. A swarm of fat bluebottle flies flowed from it, circled to form a column and then flew

231

down into the reactor. No sooner were they gone than the image dissolved into invisibility.

"That's what Yoland was doing when I was in detention," Pip said. "He was calling up . . ."

"We must divest Yoland of the spell keys," Sebastian declared. "Use your powers as punitors. We are three and he but one."

"No choice," Tim said. "Are we ready?"

The others nodded.

As one, they ran at Yoland, punching the encircling Scrottons out of the way. Several fled up the walls, chattering like angry monkeys. One fell to the ground and deflated. Sebastian closed on Yoland. For a few moments, they tussled before Sebastian was able to snatch the envelope from Yoland"s pocket.

Some of the spell keys fell out to clink on the floor. A Scrotton ran to gather them up. Tim kicked out at it, his feet meeting the Scrotton's jaw. There was a castanet-like clack as his teeth smashed into each other. Yoland tried to regain the envelope but Sebastian, after taking a few of the spell keys, threw it to Tim.

"Take a handful each," Sebastian shouted. "Throw them hard at the walls."

Pip and Tim did so. As the keys hit the reactor hall walls, they exploded in the most beautiful stark colors. Emerald, yellow, aquamarine, scarlet and violet sparks sprayed out from them, more vibrant than any firework display.

The reactor hall door opened and Loudacre entered, his face blotched by the gas from the fire extinguisher. The backs of his hands were raw, and one of his eyes was weeping badly. The other was half closed. His lips looked chapped, his forehead as red as if he had caught too much sun.

Pip, seeing him, put the spell keys she still had into her pocket.

Lurching clumsily, Loudacre staggered towards Yoland, his arms flailing in front of him. He gripped the chemistry teacher to steady himself, but this threw them both off balance. They stumbled several paces backward. At the opening into the reactor, Loudacre lost his footing.

"He's going in!" Tim muttered.

Loudacre slid slowly downward, pulling on Yoland to save him, grasping his belt. He opened his mouth and yelled. It was an unearthly screech, part human, part animal, primeval and bestial.

Yoland tried to pry Loudacre's fingers from his belt. They were tight. He started to unfasten the buckle, but he was too late. With a jerk, Loudacre tried to raise himself, and Yoland lost his footing. As Loudacre vanished from sight, Yoland struggled to find a handhold on the surrounding panels, but they were flush with each other and offered no handles. He screamed briefly. Then he too was gone.

The Scrottons clinging to the walls started to fall off. One, hanging from the roof girders far above, lost its hold and plummeted downward to follow Yoland and Loudacre into the reactor.

Tim felt someone grip his shoulder. It was Pip.

"Look!" she said, and she held out the dosimeter attached to her shirt. The square of film, which had been clear when she first put the badge on, was now dark gray.

"Let's get out of here!" Tim yelled.

Sebastian ran over to the engineers and took away the nobles. All five men immediately came to their senses and set about replacing the cover and bringing the reactor coolant gas up to pressure. Tim took Mr. Clayton's coin. He stood up unsteadily, shaking his head to clear his brain.

Pip took the guide by the hand and led him to the exit. They went as quickly as they could down the stairway. At the reception area, the remaining members of the Atom Club cowered behind the desk.

"Have you got Scrotton there?" Tim asked Den.

"The one in a school uniform," Pip added.

"No," came the reply. Den pointed to the door leading to the visitors' car park. "He's made a run for it."

Tim slammed the main entrance door open. Scrotton was loping fast down the road towards the outer perimeter security fence, his school blazer flaring out behind him.

"Stop him!" Tim yelled at the police officers. "Shoot!"

"It's one of the school kids!" came the answer.

"It's not!" Tim shouted back. He could hardly tell the truth. "It's a terrorist! He opened the reactor. He threw little bombs about. I saw him." That at least, he thought, was a truth of sorts.

Two of the policemen raised their submachine guns.

"Halt or we open fire!" bellowed the most senior policeman, a sergeant.

Scrotton paid no heed.

"This is your last warning!"

Scrotton, weaving from side to side, kept on going.

"Fire!" ordered the sergeant.

There was a short burst of automatic gunfire. The bullets struck Scrotton, spinning him around. Beyond him, the slugs ricocheted off the road surface.

"Hold your fire!"

The staccato chatter stopped abruptly. Their weapons at the ready, the policemen advanced down the road. Tim kept up with them, a few meters to their rear.

Scrotton lay in the middle of the road, one arm bent under his body, his head to one side. His eyes were open and staring. Where the bullets had hit him, there were ragged holes in the material of his school uniform.

"Oh, my God!" one of the policemen muttered, closing the safety catch on his sub-machine gun. "I've shot a child."

Yet, as the policeman spoke, Scrotton sat bolt upright.

"You shouldn't've messed with me," he growled loudly.

At that, with a detonation no louder than a small firework, his body imploded and evaporated into thin air. All that remained was a wisp of smoke, soon to be blown away on a light sea breeze.

"What the hell was that!" the police sergeant exclaimed.

The four officers went to the spot where Scrotton's body had lain. On the tarmac there was not so much as the slightest trace of blood.

Pip and Sebastian caught up with Tim while the rest of the Atom Club milled around the school minibus, not knowing what to do.

"We've lost our chauffeur," quipped Tim. "Think any of them know how to drive?"

Pip was about to reply when she heard a slight fizzing sound and looked off to her left.

Behind a security fence topped with razor wire stood a row of huge transformers from which trailed thick, high-tension cables. These in turn led to the first of a series of massive pylons at least fifty meters high. Others fanned out over the landscape in the direction of distant low hills.

For a length of about five meters, one of the cables was bulging, the swelling moving slowly towards the transformers. Pip gazed at it, bemused. It was as if the cable were a python that had just swallowed a rabbit.

Then it dawned on her. When Yoland fell into the reactor, he must have still had in his possession a set of spell keys.

"He's done it!" she screamed at Sebastian and Tim. "Look!"

She pointed to the cable. The bulge was picking up speed, heading for the transformer. Around it sizzled and danced a haze of green sparks.

Pip sprinted down the security fence, keeping up with the bulge. Tim and Sebastian followed on her heels.

By the time she reached a police Land Rover parked against the perimeter fence, she knew what she had to do. Or at least attempt. It came to her like a revelation.

She clambered onto the hood of the police vehicle and then hoisted herself onto the roof, breaking one of the windshield wipers on the way.

"Oi!" the sergeant hollered at her. "Get down! What do you think you're doing?"

Yet Pip knew exactly what she was doing.

If each spell takes four keys, she reasoned, *what happens if you upset the balance, add a fifth into the equation . . . ?*

Standing on the vehicle roof, she fumbled in her pocket and took out one of the spell keys. Holding it between index finger and thumb, as if it were a flat stone she was going to skim across a pond, she drew her arm back and spun it at the cable. It missed.

There was, she then realized, no chance of hitting the cable, never mind the accelerating bulge running down it. She took out another spell key. It was one of those made of white gold with the ⊟O⊟ furnace sign upon it.

Wait, she told herself. Her hands shook. *Wait.*

Moving ever faster, the swelling in the cable arrived at the transformer. Pip hurled the spell key at it. The key struck the top casing and bounced on to one of the huge ceramic insulators to which the cables were connected.

At that second, the bulge reached it, too.

For a moment, nothing happened; then the transformer erupted into orange flame. A brilliant white flare shot high into the sky, screeching like a banshee. Chrome-yellow darts of light flickered about it.

As quickly as it started, so did the flare die down. The transformer continued to burn, the steel casing dripping like wax into the grass, which began to smolder.

Pip climbed down from the Land Rover roof. Tim walked over to her and helped her down.

"High five, sis!" he said jubilantly.

They jumped in the air, their right hands clapping together.

"And this is?" Sebastian inquired imperturbably.

"You'll learn, my man!" Tim retorted. "You'll learn."

Mr. and Mrs. Ledger sat in silence before the television as the *News at Ten* introductory music faded and the anchorman came on.

"Our top story tonight," he began. "A nuclear emergency at the Jasper Point power station was averted this afternoon by the swift actions of three secondary school pupils who happened to be on a guided tour of the facility at the time." The screen was filled with a wide shot of the power station. "According to an official spokesman, a cover on reactor-A was blown off, causing the release of carbon dioxide gas. The pupils not only succeeded in evacuating their fellow classmates from the danger area, but were also instrumental in containing much of the released gas within the reactor building. However, the two teachers accompanying the school party were killed. An official spokesman said this was regrettable. Both men were standing very close to the gas escape. A pupil is still missing and inquiries are continuing. The public have been reassured that there is no danger of radioactive contamination from the incident."

The picture changed to Tim, Pip and Sebastian standing by the school bus with the police officers.

"The pupils, twins Timothy and Phillipa Ledger, and their friend, Sebastian Gillette, were praised by the rescue services and power station staff for their quick thinking. Dr. Singall, headmaster of Bourne End Comprehensive School in the town of Exington, which the trio attend, stated that they were a credit to the school."

Mrs. Ledger put her arms around Pip and Sebastian. Tim, sitting in an armchair, grinned expansively.

"We're so proud of you!" she said, with a catch in her voice. She smiled at Sebastian and tousled his hair. "All three of you," she added.

"Thank you very much, Mrs. Ledg– Sandra," Sebastian replied.

The picture on the TV screen changed to a brief interview with Dr. Singall standing on the area of short lawn outside the school gates, the school name board beside him.

"This is what we expect of our pupils," he said, looking at the interviewer to one side of the camera lens. "They are a credit to their school and young people in general."

The camera focus pulled back to show the school buildings.

Tim looked at Sebastian, then at Pip, then at the television screen. They had all seen the same thing.

In his hand, Dr. Singall was clearly holding a gold noble while, in the distance, in the top branches of the horse chestnut tree across the playground, was perched a black shape.

It was definitely not a crow. For a start, it had pointed ears and yellow feet . . .

It was late afternoon. Leaves drifted down from the trees. On the river, half a dozen mallards were swimming in and out of a reed bed on the opposite bank, up-tailing in the shallows. The bulrushes had gone to seed, their mace-like heads breaking up into fluffs of gossamer drifting away on the breeze.

"Think we'll get a medal?" Tim wondered as he lowered himself down next to his sister on the bench in the Garden of Eden. Then, putting on a plummy voice, he continued, "'And what have you done, young man?' I fought off evil and saved a nuclear power station, Your Majesty. 'I say, jolly good show, what! Arise, Sir Timothy.'"

"Single-handed, was it?" Pip said sarcastically.

"Only joking," Tim assured her. "If there's medals, there will have to be three of them."

"Do you think we shall hear of Yoland again? Or de Loudéac?"

"After they've been radiated, frozen stiff and fried? I think not. That's pretty final, don't you think?"

Sebastian, who had been at the far end of the copse, approached them.

"The climate is indeed very different from my childhood," he remarked. "There are both orpine and southernwood in flower on the meadow rim. Both should bloom in July and fruit in August yet now, in late autumn, their buds are opening."

"How're you feeling?" Tim inquired.

"In what respect?"

"Don't you feel sleepy? Isn't it time to pay a trip to hibernation land?"

Sebastian sat down next to Pip. One of the mallards took to the wing, circled once over the copse and settled back on the river with the others.

"I have been considering that," Sebastian admitted. "By all intents and purposes, I should by now have withdrawn to my slumber, and yet I have no desire so to do. I have, I sense, some other matter to address."

"Dr. Singall?"

"I think not," Sebastian declared. "It is true he possesses one of Yoland's nobles, and yet I do not feel great evil surrounding him and it will exercise no power with Yoland gone." He looked out across the meadow. "This is a most beautiful location. It was ever thus is my early days."

"Strange how such beauty can hide such wickedness," Pip observed.

"It is always thus. Remember what I have said. One cannot have a light without a darkness in which to put it. Without evil, how can there be goodness?"

Pip got to her feet. The edgy mallard took to the wing again, its neck outstretched, its feet tucked in and its wings working hard to gain altitude.

"Time for tea and scones," she announced.

"And potassium iodide pills . . ." Tim went on, crinkling his nose ". . . the price of being radiated." He held up his dosimeter badge. "Now is that a souvenir or what?"

"I could perhaps prepare an alternative infusion of vulnerary herbs," Sebastian said meditatively, ". . . hare's foot, comfrey, plantain, with common kelp . . ."

The look on Pip and Tim's faces was sufficient to give Sebastian an answer.

They reached the gate by the coach house.

"So," Pip said as she opened the latch, "it seems you'll be here for a while longer."

"Indeed it does," Sebastian answered. "For better or for worse."

ꓱ Soul Stealer Reader's Guide ꓱ

Like its companion book, *Doctor Illuminatus, Soul Stealer* merges present and past and science and suspense as it explores the ancient practice of alchemy. Here are some questions that probe further into the many deep (and dark) layers of this novel.

1) Sebastian reminds Pip and Tim of the main aims of alchemy: to make a homunculus, turn common metals into gold, and achieve immortality. He mentions a number of potions and elixirs throughout the book, including *caput mortuum*, *aqua soporiferum*, *elixir vitae*, and *aurum potabile*. How does each of these terms relate to alchemy? Do you agree that alchemy has a valid purpose? Why or why not?

2) Tim describes his homeroom teacher, Yoland, as a "murderer, a mind-bender, and a traitor." How does Yoland fit each characteristic of this three-part description?

3) Pip and Tim are faced with the challenge of converting the fifteenth century–born Sebastian into a regular twenty-first-century kid. What are some of the "modern" words they teach him? Are these words still used today? Which are used in England only, and which are used in both England and the U.S.? What are some other steps Pip and Tim take when they give Sebastian a makeover? What other steps would you take to make him fit in at your school?

4) When Tim suggests to Sebastian, "Can't you sort of use magic to make your way [to school]? Turn up as a bird and change into human mode in a stall in the boys' room or behind the bike sheds?" Sebastian says that this is possible, but not wise. Describe Sebastian's powers. What kinds of responsibilities go along with using those powers? Why do you think he chooses not to follow Tim's suggestion, but cures Julia of her warts?

5) Sebastian alludes to several figures from British history, including Queen Elizabeth, Queen Victoria, Queen Anne, Queen Joan, the Duke of Gloucester, Henry IV, and Henry V. Based on the descriptions of these figures from the text — and on your own research — which is the most interesting figure to you? Why?

6) Sebastian describes to Tim and Pip some ancient medicinal practices used in his father's time. Since it was believed that noxious odors caused disease — and that the risk of infection was reduced if they could be counteracted with a pleasant smell — people carried lemons and other fruit with them, often pierced with cloves, to produce a strong and beneficial scent. Sebastian also mentions that a powder of dessicated sowbugs taken with warm milk was used to help ease stomachaches. What unusual ancient medicinal practices can you think of that are used today?

7) Sebastian tells Pip that what she sees through the camera obscura is her chimera, "the beast of your fears and nightmares." What other meanings of "chimera" are

mentioned in the book? Look up "chimera" in the dictionary — what different meanings of the word do you find there?

8) When Tim goes fishing, he is startled to see not one but several Scrottons. Sebastian explains that, like a butterfly, replicates of the original Scrotton emerge from the shell of a chrysalis. How does this process of creating replicates of one species compare to the process of cloning as we know it today? In your opinion, what are the positive and negative effects of creating replicates/cloning in this book and in real life?

9) Sebastian's father's enemy, Malodor, has a name that is a pun (a play on words revealing different senses of the same word): it means "bad smell" in French, and this description is fitting for his evil character. Malodor is also called de Loudéac and Loudacre. Do these aliases also reflect his character? In what ways do you feel that Pip (whose real name is Phillipa), Tim (or Timothy), Sebastian, Guy Scrotton, or other characters have names that fit their personalities or roles in the book?

10) Do you believe in spellbooks and spellkeys? Does the evidence in this book convince you that such devices exist? Why or why not? Do you believe that one day, there will be a way to read people's minds? To control — or steal — their souls?

Dangerous magic — ancient enemies

Doctor Illuminatus

Sebastian is the alchemist's son,
pursuing his father's enemies
through the centuries.

Caught in a web of magic and
cunning, Pip and Tim's only hope
of escape is to join the desperate battle
against unimaginable evil.

The first book about the alchemist's son —
a fantastical tale of sorcery and betrayal